# SISTER MORPHINE OF CORRECTION

by

MARIA ANGELO

CHIMERA

Sister Murdock's House of Correction
first published in 2000 by
Chimera Publishing Ltd
PO Box 152
Waterlooville
Hants
PO8 9FS


Printed and bound in Great Britain by
Omnia Books Limited, Glasgow


This book is sold subject to the condition that it shall not, by way of trade or otherwise, be lent, resold, hired out or otherwise circulated without the publisher's prior written consent in any form of binding or cover other than that in which it is published, and without a similar condition being imposed on the subsequent purchaser.


The characters and situations in this book are entirely imaginary and bear no relation to any real person or actual happening.


Copyright © Maria Angelo

The right of Maria Angelo to be identified as author of this book has been asserted in accordance with section 77 and 78 of the Copyrights Designs and Patents Act 1988

# SISTER MURDOCK'S HOUSE OF CORRECTION

Maria Angelo

This novel is fiction – in real life practice safe sex

# Chapter One

I am twenty years old, yet I still think of myself as a little girl. I look at the world around me, so full of sexual innuendoes and hidden meanings, and it always seems that everyone knows what's going on except me. Yet I know I'm not stupid – just a little too trusting. I suppose I shouldn't complain. Despite my naïvety, I've done pretty well for myself. After all, I am married to a multi-millionaire.

From the very first time I met Sir Peter Easton, and long before I had any realistic prospects of marriage, I daydreamed about the possibility of me, Sarah Singleton, a complete nonentity, becoming his wife. The advantages and the sheer esteem of such a position were obvious. But my fantasies were so intense that it amused me to consider even the possible drawbacks. I would have to play second fiddle to his business commitments for sure, and that could mean serious boredom while he was away. I knew there would be begging letters to answer and invasion of privacy by photographers. I was certainly scared that I would find myself completely out of my depth socially.

But it simply never occurred to me that my major problem would be sex.

I must admit that sex is a subject that has always been something of a puzzle to me. I'd strongly resent anyone suggesting that I was frigid or unemotional. In fact, I've had plenty of indications that in truth I'm easily inclined to overheat. But I would have to admit that I find it confusing, to put things mildly, and confusion frequently gives the impression of reluctance. My very first excursion into the murky world of sex illustrates this ambivalence perfectly.

It was during one of the school holidays, just after my sixteenth birthday. Things started innocently enough. As I undressed for bed in the privacy of my own room I became interested in my breasts. They were already well shaped and aggressive and I was fascinated by them, as any girl would be. On more than one occasion I'd noticed several envious glances in the school changing rooms.

'Warm and inviting,' I murmured under my breath without really knowing what I meant, although there was clearly more than a grain of truth in comparison with the miserable, angry little pimples some girls my age still sported.

I touched the nipples tentatively and puzzled over the way they grew hard. It was oddly exciting and I wanted to show the effect to someone, but of course I was far too self-conscious to be able to do so.

It happened that the nextdoor cat, a tabby called Moggy, mewed at my window at that moment. He used to climb up a nearby tree and along the roof of our garage, and I could never resist letting him in. He rubbed himself against my legs in a way I found quite erotic.

'Look at my nipples, Moggy,' I whispered, proudly. 'Aren't they big?'

He took no notice, of course, and I felt somewhat let down. Then I had an absurd idea, but one so outrageous I simply had to try it. I put my night-dress on, crept down to the kitchen, and got some cream out of the fridge. Back upstairs I offered a little to Moggy on the end of my finger. He went completely mad, slavering away at my hand long after the cream was all gone. And his tongue rasped like sandpaper.

Nervously I took my night-dress off again and lay on my back on the bed, naked. Appalled at what I was doing I allowed a dollop of cream to drip onto my right breast. The cat fell upon it avidly. I almost screamed in shock as his tongue tore across the tender surface. I gripped the sides of the bed desperately and closed my eyes in erotic wonder as he continued to lick over and around the now rampant bud. This moment marked the first time I lost my self-control and an unsuppressed groan escaped from my throat. I heard the living room door open downstairs and then there was silence as my father listened, puzzled.

'Anything wrong, Sarah?' he called up.

'No, no,' I answered, voice still choked with emotion. 'I just dropped something on my big toe.'

Downstairs the door closed again, and I let my breath out at last. My right nipple was on fire and was tingling fiercely but I couldn't make up my mind whether it was from pain or pleasure. The poor over-stimulated thing could obviously stand no more excitement, so I gave the left one a generous helping of cream and lay there trying not to whimper as the cat continued the strange torture I had invented. In due course my whole body became suffused with a strange agitation, a little like pins and needles, and the feeling ran out into my arms and legs like water. I heard myself gasping with what seemed like breathlessness, even though I was doing nothing the slightest bit energetic, and all at once I appeared to wet myself. I reached down and found that the coverlet was still dry enough, but I was horrified to find that between my legs was an inexplicable surfeit of moisture that seemed to suggest that something biologically unpleasant had occurred. At that moment I heard my parents talking in the hall on their way upstairs to bed and I hurriedly pushed Moggy back out onto the windowsill and dived into bed.

I was extremely scared and I never tried the same trick again, being fearful at the time that I had caused myself some injury, some internal rupture that would return to haunt me in the future.

From then on and right up to my marriage I remained absurdly naïve. Mothers are traditionally supposed to draw their daughters aside on wedding mornings to offer a few well-chosen words on what to expect between the sheets that night. And, if we are to believe the Victorians, even to advise the prospective bride in extremis to 'lie back and think of England'. Mine offered me no such insight, nor even the expected advice on contraception. I imagine she hoped that I knew absolutely nothing of such matters and would therefore fall pregnant on the very first night, presenting her in due course with a grandchild which would then, by virtue of its surname, irrevocably seal my bond with Sir Peter, incidentally ensuring its grandmother a comfortable and secure old age.

Instead my mother crammed down my throat all sorts of irrelevant exhortations I could happily have done without. Like her, I still didn't really believe this wedding was actually happening and I was, as can well be understood, petrified with fear at the thought of committing some social gaffe.

'For goodness sake remember that you will become *Lady Sarah*,' she warned me, 'and don't scratch your nose in view of any of the photographers.'

What a singularly unhelpful remark! She was treating me like the child I secretly believed I was. I was an adult, I reminded myself, and I didn't need my mother to tell me not to pick my nose. But at the same time such a comment only helped to remind me that it was exactly the catastrophic sort of mistake I might actually make in the heat of the moment while concentrating on my marriage vows or what cutlery to use at dinner. The Queen, I reflected enviously, has a lifetime to learn the art of protecting her image in public. I had to get it right first time. However, in the event, the wedding ceremony passed off perfectly. Even the normally ill-mannered media was unstinting in its admiration. In my $10,000 Ermio Urbani dress the local television station that evening called me 'an enchanting English rose, as fresh and innocent as spring'. My mother loved that, of course. But I had serious misgivings. It sounded as though they had already guessed my guilty secret.

A couple of the cheaper tabloids had earlier been impolite enough to describe me as 'a checkout girl made good'. This incensed my mother who seemed quite prepared to take them to court for slander. But I realised the remark was not meant vindictively. They counted a large number of checkout girls in their readership and wanted merely to emphasise that even though you might be ordinary there was still some hope for you in the rat race of life. Of course they were wildly inaccurate on two accounts. Firstly I was never a checkout girl but rather a trainee store manager with an expensive Westover College education behind me, and secondly, even within that definition, I was far from ordinary. Despite my inner terror, when I looked in the mirror on my wedding morning I actually giggled as I remembered an old joke: 'I used to be conceited but now I'm perfect'. A child I might feel but in looks, at least, I had nothing to be ashamed of. I was all grown up; my hair a radiant auburn, my face a bewitchingly oval picture of virtue, my body a heart-stopping ten on any scale.

I told myself vainly that it was difficult to imagine anyone less comparable to a checkout girl. That evening I would be flying, by private jet of course, to St Kitts with my new husband, to spend our honeymoon in a house owned by one of Sir Peter's business associates and at one time used as a meeting place for heads of state during the Bay of Pigs crisis. And then, a week later, we would be returning to take up residence in Finchington Yardley, one of the few stately homes left in England not made over for tax purposes in perpetuity to The National Trust. Thereafter I would live a life of ease, not to say obscene luxury, my every whim pampered.

And here's a twist. Sir Peter was not, as will have been assumed, a man of advanced years and distended stomach, with a dripping nose and a tobacco-stained silver moustache. He was extremely handsome and young; a mere twenty-five, as vigorous as his age implied, and with a string of thriving supermarkets sporting his name. On my wedding day there was not a single reason, as far as I could see, for every woman in the country not to feel bitterly jealous of me, an object of hatred of the entire female population of Great Britain. I should have loved it, of course, but I remained miserably apprehensive, certain that somewhere someone would expose me for what I was.

For me the wedding was marred by only two things. The first was that my nose itched all day with a hateful persistence that I blamed on my mother's earlier remark. The second was my dreadful secret.

I was still a virgin.

To be sure, the essence of my good looks is freshness. My eyes are deep blue pools of innocence, my lips rich red innocent cherries waiting to be plucked, my cheeks sport a perpetual innocent blush, and my neck is a long vulnerable pillar of innocence, pointing downward to soft innocent shoulders and pert innocent breasts that beg male hands to caress and ultimately defile their innocence in a savage orgy of bestial lust. There wasn't a girl in the whole of Britain that looked more like a virgin than I did.

But of course nobody expected me actually to *be* one. On the single occasion I had stayed overnight at Sir Peter's town house in Mayfair after an evening at the theatre I was expecting to be deflowered, and although I was scared I privately welcomed the idea. I had to get it over with, had been my overriding sentiment. But I stumbled dizzily as he ushered me through the door and that had revealed my extreme nervousness. In response, Peter behaved as the perfect gentleman, giving me my own room to sleep in. But that hadn't stopped the papers printing pictures of us leaving together the following morning, with the obvious implication that we were now lovers.

I survived the wedding and the interminable reception afterwards without any visible social gaffes. I even enjoyed our transatlantic flight through the night hours with Peter hugging my arm. But as I undressed for bed in the bathroom of our suite, and put on the deliciously naughty piece of froth that Alicia Salons had described as 'the quintessential honeymoon nightie', I was trembling with fear and apprehension.

Peter was a real person, polite and reserved.

I was a real person, with private thoughts and private fears.

How could the two of us suddenly cavort about naked, like animals, invading each other's bodies and minds? It didn't seem reasonable. The contrast with the afternoon's formal wedding reception was far too great.

So why doesn't every newlywed couple suffer from this problem? In my case it's possible that my reluctance was initiated by the particular events that took place in Greece some three years earlier when I was seventeen. That was the age and the occasion when I should have lost my virginity to an anonymous stranger. I failed, and indeed ultimately behaved so badly that the episode seemed to have left me with a genuine guilt-complex about sex. I was now seriously concerned that, against my own wishes, I would fight Peter off. I recalled an embarrassing experience when I was about ten. I had a very painful tooth that kept me awake for hours at night. One single visit to the dentist could cure all that, my mother convinced me. I must simply grit my teeth and endure the relatively short period of suffering that implied. But in the event I fought like a wild cat. I could not even bear the man's fingers inside my mouth, let alone the drill. Very soon he lost his patience with me.

'Perhaps you should come back when she is less overwrought,' was what he said to my mother.

Well, overwrought was what I felt now. If I had been scared of a man putting his fingers inside my mouth, what was I to make of the awful prospect that now faced me? Peter was about to force his manhood right inside my private parts.

Was my poor little unstretched honey-pot capable of accepting such violence?

How big would his member be? How heavy would he feel, lying on top of me? How violent would his lust be? Would he desist if I cried out with pain?

A girl should not brood on such things on her wedding night. She should just let it happen. But if my fear of invasion was serious enough I was also absurdly terrified of the other extreme – overreaction. I thought back on my behaviour with Moggy, the cat. Would I lose my self-control, as I'd been led to believe many women did during the sex act? It was contradictory, of course, that I was at the same time frightened of not liking sex, and frightened of liking it too much. But that was in truth exactly how I felt. I was biologically a virgin, and that gave me a great sense of fear and inadequacy. But I also knew, because I'd experienced them first hand three years before, that there were lots of things that a man and a woman could do to each other which could feel sexy, or scary, or painful, or exciting. Too exciting. Here I was, with a man I hardly knew, in a house full of servants who were listening behind every door, ready to react to our every whim, and with the world's press waiting outside for any juicy titbits they could feed to their readers. How could I possibly relax and be myself? I'd been fighting to retain my composure all day. Night had arrived and I was still fighting.

I had already taken far too long to get ready. Nervously

I turned the handle of the bathroom door and stepped into the bedroom. Peter was sitting up in bed waiting for me. I felt his eyes upon me as I took the half-dozen steps across the room. Porcelain, I told myself. I must think of myself as a porcelain doll, delicate and precious, lovely to look at and touch, but entirely dead.

Whatever was to ensue, I must just let it happen.

I climbed into my side of the bed, eyes lowered.

'You're trembling,' said Peter. 'There's no need to be nervous. Honestly.'

Although I was scared I didn't like the considerate tone of his voice. For heaven's sake don't be nice to me, I thought. I'd far rather be taken savagely. Then it'd be over and done with. Don't prolong the agony.

'We don't have to do it, you know,' he continued.

'Yes we do,' I said, far too quickly.

'All right,' Peter said, 'but you're as white as a sheet. Please relax. Don't forget, you can stop me at any time.'

When Peter moved on top of me I gave a little gasp of anticipation.

Immediately concern showed again in his eyes and he hesitated, afraid of frightening me.

'Look, Sarah, I'll stop. We're both tired. We've had an appallingly long day.'

'No,' I said, 'just do it.'

That sounded about as romantic as a patient telling the doctor to give her a tetanus shot. Let's just get it over with.

My trembling had by now become almost uncontrollable. I gripped the bedclothes in a vain attempt to keep my body still, and even clamped the corner of the pillow between my teeth, just like a sailor on Nelson's

*Victory* biting a bullet while his leg is being amputated.

'It's all right, pet,' he said. 'That's enough for now.'

Ever the gentleman. I should, of course, have demanded that he finish what he had begun, but I was too much of a coward. All I could think of was that I had survived night number one unscathed.

Or maybe not.

As I lay next to Peter's sleeping body and my initial relief wore off I reflected on what this disaster implied. I couldn't possibly assume that Peter had enjoyed our first attempt at lovemaking. We had got absolutely nowhere!

He had just spent several hundred thousand pounds on a sumptuous wedding and committed his name to some little nobody whose only merit was that her body looked as though it would fuck like a rabbit, only to find that in the crunch she'd totally failed to come across with the goods.

Men had to get satisfaction from sex, I knew. Otherwise they would go and find it elsewhere. It may seem odd that I was already considering Peter's possible infidelity on our wedding night, but the reason was clear. Some men are painfully reserved, almost to the point of impotence. It's just those sort of men that marry – if they can afford it – the sexy-looking girls in the hope of being stimulated out of their restraint. My earlier conceit before the wedding had come from the sure knowledge that I had the prettiest face, the longest legs, and the perkiest bosom available.

Yet I had manifestly failed to satisfy him, or even bring him to an orgasm!

In retrospect I realised that I should at least have offered to do it with my mouth. That was, after all, the one sex act I was familiar with.

But of course, I had been far too self-conscious to suggest a simple solution like that.

Having slept only intermittently I awoke late the following morning. Peter had already got up – out jogging, probably, before the sun became too hot. I used the phone to order us both breakfast and had the waiter take it out on the veranda. Apprehensive after the problems of the previous night, I was relieved that in this small domestic chore at least my timing was perfect; Peter arrived just as our melon and smoked kippers did.

After a quick shower he joined me as I gazed out over the immaculate shrub-lined lawn which fell gradually away to reveal a startlingly blue sea in the distance. He planted a kiss on the back of my neck and I poured him some coffee. He was far too polite to bring up the subject of my failure the previous night. But I knew I had to get it out into the open.

'Peter… about last night,' I said apprehensively. 'I'm really very sorry I was so nervous—'

He waved a hand dismissively. 'Oh, don't worry about it,' he said. 'Worrying only makes things worse. I'm sure it will work out fine in due course. There's no hurry.'

That was clearly supposed to reassure me. And maybe that's the right thing to do with someone who has a serious psychological hang-up. But unfortunately it made me think of a possibility so blatantly obvious that I couldn't imagine why it hadn't dawned on me before. I have the kind of looks people admire; fashion magazine material, the ideal body that every woman wants. But I wasn't so foolish as to imagine that was the same thing as having the ideal body for a man intent on sex. Suppose Peter secretly craved a slut with a huge bosom?

He wouldn't marry one; that wouldn't suit his public image. But then a man with his sort of money didn't have to. He could get whatever kind of woman he wanted, whenever he wanted, just by paying for it.

So maybe he didn't want me for sex, he just wanted me as an ornament! No wonder he was so polite and forbearing. He simply didn't care.

He had jokingly warned me that I would have to play the part of Lady Sarah Easton to the full once we were back at Finchington. For instance, when important foreign visitors came to stay. Like any other girl I was excited by the prospect and more than willing to work hard at the part. But not if that was all I was to be. I shuddered at the prospect of having to turn a blind eye to any affairs Peter chose to indulge in, while remaining myself whiter than white.

One problem was that Peter was an extremely accomplished actor – along with the million other things he was good at. He was well known for his support of the theatre, and some small percentage of his fortune was directed into avant-garde ventures in which he sometimes, but not always, took part. These plays always drew the highest critical acclaim, as did his performances. And it wasn't just lip service from sycophants. He was genuinely brilliant, damn him. I would never be able to tell when he was deceiving me.

This line of thought reminded me that he had been romantically linked a couple of years earlier to an actress called Susanna Monk. He had taken me to Drury Lane one evening to see her in an outrageous presentation of *The Servant* by Harold Pinter. I felt out of my depth and puzzled by some of the play's implications, but I could not deny that Susanna was brilliant. And beautiful. I thought at the time that maybe I could just out-point her on looks – after all, she was at least seven or eight years older than me. But given her obvious intelligence and talent I felt more than a little threatened by her.

At dinner afterwards I jokingly asked Peter whether there had been any truth in the romantic rumours. His reply, though offered light-heartedly, chilled me to the marrow.

'I'm not going to answer that,' he said. 'If you were a newspaper reporter you would take that as an excuse to announce that your suspicions had been confirmed. But that would be wrong. There are times when it's better to deflect questions long before they get too close – before a refusal to reply becomes an admission of guilt.'

So on that situation, as on many others, I had failed to get inside his mind. And in just such a vein our honeymoon passed. Peter was never anything less than totally polite and solicitous. He made sure I knew I could ask for and get anything I wanted. In return, he expected me to give him freedom to enjoy pastimes for which I had felt no interest, such as golf or deep-sea fishing.

Although he attempted to make love to me on several subsequent occasions he gave up as soon as it became obvious that I was still terrified. The result was, however, that we returned to England from St Kitts still, in some odd sense, strangers.

# Chapter Two

So for Sarah the innocent young child things looked pretty bleak. I was too hung-up to surrender my virginity to Peter, and he was too polite to take it by force. And, horror of horrors, in his plan of things maybe it didn't matter too much.

But it mattered like hell to me.

You read about people with mental hang-ups and you wonder why they don't just stop whinging and start living, like everyone else. But when it happens to you it's not so easy to behave rationally.

The obvious course of action should have been to go to an expensive psychoanalyst and have myself 'shrunk', or whatever the correct term is. But I absolutely could not do that. Peter and I were far too well known. Any one of the seedier newspapers would pay a huge sum of money to be able to report that our wedding had not been consummated. Even if I found an analyst with impeccable morals – and I'd no idea how to do that – someone would be sure to photograph me going into his or her clinic, and then the fat would be in the fire.

I began to look back on my period of self-enforced celibacy – the three years after my Greek holiday – as seriously wasted time. I had been so appalled by the final outcome of my spree in Lindos that I had deliberately fought off all invitations to bed afterwards. It had made me feel self-righteous and virtuous. But now I could see that my peculiar behaviour had turned me into a very unusual individual; one with the looks of a very expensive whore but with all the practical knowledge of a six-year-old.

Well, the first step to enlightenment was obviously self-analysis. After years of deliberately suppressing the memories I decided it was now high time I thought through my earlier Greek escapade, in the hope that self-contemplation might lead to an explanation as to why I was still so overwrought whenever Peter made his approaches. Why pay a psychiatrist two hundred pounds an hour when maybe all you need is some honesty?

The events I'm referring to took place on the idyllic Greek Island of Rhodes.

It was to Lindos, the island's foremost tourist trap, where, at the tender age of seventeen, I had gone on a package holiday with Megan, my best friend from Westover School. My parents would probably have forked out for me to go further afield, but Megan was struggling to find the cash, even for a cheapie to Greece, and she so desperately wanted me to go with her that I could not refuse.

I certainly didn't intend to yield up my virginity during the holiday. Although Megan and I were quite prepared to adopt boyfriends for the duration of our stay, we did not expect the physical side of the relationship to go beyond an arm around the waist and a few stolen kisses. At that stage in my development boys were all right for going on walks with, or being admired by, or to discuss on the beach, but one really didn't want their hands poking around where they didn't belong.

However, that very first balmy night all but thwarted

my plans, and there was worse to come later. This may sound like the familiar story of the swarthy Latin lover, a perfect romantic evening under twinkling Mediterranean stars, a vine-covered restaurant, followed by a walk along the beach, waves gently lapping from a wine-dark sea, with Prince Charming by my side. Nothing so romantic, I'm afraid, although of wine, I must admit, there was plenty.

On our first afternoon Megan and I lay out on the beach, under the famous Lindos acropolis, soaking up the unfamiliar sun. Megan was topless, but of course I didn't have the nerve to copy her.

'Don't be such a silly,' she said to me. 'Take your bra off.'

I shook my head miserably. 'I can't.'

'Course you can!' she insisted. 'Be bare or be square. This is Greece, and we're here to relax.'

'How can I possibly be relaxed if I'm stark naked on a crowded beach?' I asked.

'Don't exaggerate,' she admonished. 'It's only your top, for God's sake. Everybody does it. Look, I'm sweating with embarrassment at lying beside someone who's so out of touch.'

At the time I was puzzled by her insistence, but on the other hand it was just what I needed. Secretly I liked the idea of doing something my parents would find so outrageous. But without her pushing I wouldn't have had the nerve.

At last, swallowing hard, I reached behind my back, undid the clasp, and tossed away the thin strip of material. I was then overwhelmed by a desire to lie down immediately on my stomach. But that would only have emphasised my gaucheness. I had to tough it out. Trembling, I lay on my back, covering my face with the book I had brought along to read.

I lay there listening to the murmur of voices on the beach and to the comings and goings of the sun worshippers, hoping they were taking no notice of me.

'Jesus, Simon, check out the tits on that angel over there!' I heard.

The upper-class English accent cut through the groundswell of noise. Were they talking about me? I couldn't possibly tell, at least not without deliberately looking in their direction, announcing my interest. But I believed so, whether or not it was true. My breasts started to tingle. I could feel all the eyes on the beach staring at them. Sweat was trickling down my nose.

Recalling the strange episode with the cat, Moggy, I peaked nervously downwards under the edge of the book and my worst fears were realised.

Unbidden twin turrets stood to attention on my breasts, like sturdy little Martello towers, two sentries standing guard over my treasures. Suppressing a whimper of misery I rolled quickly onto my stomach.

Time passed in silence, and then Megan lifted herself up on one elbow. 'You are lucky, you know,' she said suddenly.

'Why?' I asked, puzzled.

'All the men look at you,' she said.

I had been doggedly avoiding catching the eye of any of our neighbours.

'How do you know it's not you they're staring at?' I replied, tangentially.

'Don't be silly,' she said. 'They never do. I haven't got

anything worth looking at.'

'Your breasts are bigger than mine,' I protested, chiefly to find something to say.

'But not as nice,' she answered. 'Besides, it's not your breasts they're staring at.'

'What else is there?' I enquired, genuinely naïve.

'Your bum, silly,' she said.

I couldn't believe what I'd heard. 'What?' I said. 'You're joking! A bum's something to sit on. That's all.'

'No it's not,' she argued. 'Men go gaga over them. Mine's a disaster. Too low, too flabby.'

'Megan, you're out of your mind,' I said. 'A bum's a bum. That's all.'

'Huh,' she snorted. 'Your bum is your passport to success and fortune. It's a peach, Sally.'

'Nonsense!' I exclaimed. 'I simply don't believe you.'

The silly conversation had graduated to the status of a stand-off.

Megan thought for a minute, and then said, 'We can prove it.'

'How?' I was intrigued.

'First of all we'll lie on our backs, right?' she suggested.

I glanced down hurriedly and was relieved to see that the sentries had mercifully gone off duty.

'All right,' I concurred carefully.

We rolled onto our backs, holding our paperbacks above our eyes to shut out some of the blinding sun. I tried to remain as inconspicuous as possible, but I noticed that Megan's super-structure wandered around quite disgracefully, and I had the impression she was deliberately exaggerating its waywardness by fussing and fidgeting into a comfortable position. We waited a couple of minutes.

'Okay, now count how many blokes are looking at us,' she said.

'How can we do that?' I asked.

She tutted impatiently and said, 'Easy. Pretend to be reading, first with your head on one side, then the other. But look over the edge of your book and count the eyes.'

I was trembling with self-consciousness, but even so I had to admit it was fun. 'God, this is creepy,' I said. 'I can't work out whether that ginger-haired one is locked onto us or whether he's reading too. He's got sun-specs on.'

'We'll count him in,' she said enthusiastically. 'That makes seven, by my reckoning.'

'Seven pairs, fourteen lascivious eyes,' I confirmed.

'Right,' she went on determinedly. 'Now over onto our fronts.'

With relief I did as she instructed. It was more difficult to scan the beach from that position, but not impossible.

'Five pairs,' I said, with an I-told-you-so voice. 'Your boobs have it over my buttocks.'

'We're not finished yet,' she countered. 'My boobs are bare. Your buttocks are covered.'

'Well I'm certainly not taking my bottom half off too, if that's what you're thinking!' I insisted indignantly.

'No need,' she said calmly. 'Just pull the material up as if you're trying to get your cheeks tanned.'

'I can't do that!' I said.

'Course you can,' she urged. 'I'll do it for you. I'll put sun oil on them.'

She sat up, tugged my bathing costume upward till it was all crammed into the cleft between my buttocks, and she then proceeded to smear me with expensive oil. I thought she took longer over it than necessary, but I supposed she was trying to attract an audience.

'Okay,' she said, flopping back down next to me. 'Now we'll count again.'

It was awesome. As I watched an old guy with a crotchety wife manoeuvred himself round on his stomach so he could see me.

'Thirteen,' I admitted, quietly.

'There you are,' Megan said triumphantly. 'What did I tell you?'

I couldn't see why she was so pleased at being proved right, but right she was, and there was a strange bubbly feeling in my stomach as I surveyed the effect I'd had on the somnolent Greek beach. This is power, I told myself.

How very peculiar. How very unexpected.

Although all those eyes were staring at us, there was thankfully still something impersonal about the situation. I told myself we could still pretend we were two sun worshippers soaking up the healthy rays, oblivious to any effects we might be having. But pretty soon these two young bucks wandered over to talk to us.

'Didn't we see you on the plane on the way over?' one said. 'BA812 from Gatwick?'

Big deal – it was a package holiday, what else did they expect? However, Megan was suitably impressed.

'Yes, we were on that plane,' she squealed. 'Are you from England then? What a coincidence!'

And so on.

She rolled over onto her back to indicate her interest. I stayed on my front, recently made aware that I might be doing more for my image in that position.

Actually, the two lads weren't too bad looking. We

learned that their names were Piers and Simon – evidently the unseen breast-admiring voices – and they were plainly yuppies; stockbroker material slumming it on a package deal till their ship came in. When they asked us whether we'd care to join them for a nice Greek meal that evening I was happy enough to accept, though not quite as effusive about it as Megan.

My expectations were modest. I imagined we would make up a foursome for the rest of our stay, sunbathing together, going on the obligatory tourist excursions, eventually holding hands under the table in the bars, and maybe even kissing in the moonlight before parting in great sorrow to go our separate ways at the end of the holiday. But it occurred to me halfway through the meal that things weren't going to be that straightforward. We were on someone's roof – they don't have enough space on the streets to swing a cat and all the restaurants have expanded vertically. In fact, that's where the cats were too, rubbing against our legs, begging for titbits, the gristle from the moussaka or the skin from the sole.

It was dark, warm, and the air was heavily scented with jasmine. Idyllic, as I said. We should have already been paired off and holding hands. Major problem: our two suitors did not seem to have decided which of us would go with which. Appalling etiquette. Instead they were both staring at me with the sort of dangerous glint in their eyes that men get before they eat the cream out of a chocolate eclair.

I admit I behaved reprehensibly, and with few excuses. Okay, I was tired from the flight and from having had to get up at five in the morning for the journey to Gatwick from Chislehurst where I lived. And I drank too much wine – far too much. Retsina is ridiculously cheap, and although it tastes filthy you forget about that after the first glass. At about eleven o'clock, when I no longer knew which way was up, Megan excused herself to go to the toilet.

Before I knew what was happening the lads had paid the bill and I found myself staggering down a narrow winding Greek street supported by two lusty over-excited males, one on my left and one on my right, each with his fingers surreptitiously tickling the underside of a bewildered breast. Good thing I put a bra on before coming out, I remember my soggy brain thinking, before it realised that somewhere along the walk home my breasts and their bra had regrettably become separated.

That was probably my last coherent thought. From then on my brain disassociated itself in disgust from my body and watched the rest of the night's frolics from somewhere several feet above my head. It saw me being half-carried up rickety wooden steps to the boys' shared room. It saw them roll and then pass round a strange-looking cigarette, with me always getting the lion's share of the smoke, and then it saw me collapse slowly onto their bed and drift off into a coma.

Now this is odd, I thought. If I've passed out, how is it I still know what's going on? I think it must have been one of those psychic out-of-body experiences people have when they nearly die under anaesthetic. My brain had plainly lost the ability to move any of my limbs, or even to open my eyes for me, but some little glowing core at the centre of its being still hung tenaciously to awareness, viewing the proceedings with a certain wry humour, almost of *déjà vu*.

I felt fingers on the front of my shirt and then a cool breeze informed me that my buppies were now enjoying the open air.

'Christ, they're beautiful,' said Piers, in awe.

'She's a living doll,' replied Simon, with much more urgency in his voice.

'Come on, help me get her shirt off.' Piers again.

This is nice, I thought. These lads are talking about me with genuine admiration. It's gratifying to be appreciated.

But somewhere a deeper, more fundamental part of my primitive defence system told me that admiration might not be all I would get that evening. But there didn't seem to be anything I could do about it.

'Sarah, can you hear me?' Simon whispered in my ear.

Of course I could.

'She's passed out,' he announced eagerly. 'She can't feel a thing.'

Simon's hands descended onto my defenceless rosebuds and started squeezing and pulling the flesh as if he were a baker kneading dough at piece rate.

Ouch, I thought, as I realised that my poor white Northern European breasts had been savagely treated by the afternoon's Southern European sun.

Lips took the place of hands and were somewhat less painful, though much more personal. Oh Lord, I thought, my nipples were doing something they shouldn't.

'Does that mean she's awake?' said Piers, clearly referring to the twin towers that were proclaiming my involvement.

'No, not at all,' said Simon. 'It's a conditioned reflex.'

'Can I have a go?' Piers asked.

'I thought you wanted to chicken out,' mocked Simon.

'Can't do any harm, just to have a suck,' said Piers, defensively.

I was saving those for my first baby, I remembered, unable to fight them off.

'Come on,' Simon growled impatiently. 'Get her jeans off.'

'We shouldn't be doing this,' said cautious Piers.

Damn right they shouldn't, I thought.

'I didn't hear you complaining when we took Fiona Hollingsworth in tandem,' said Simon.

'That was different,' Piers said defensively. 'She's anybody's. Besides, she was begging for it.'

'So is this girl,' Simon decreed. 'We didn't force her to come out with us or to drink all that wine. She's expecting to be laid.'

'Not insensible, she's not,' Piers countered.

But a pair of clumsy hands was pulling down my jeans, and then my briefs. And since another pair was still busy mauling my super-structure it was clear that Piers' reluctance was only lip service. Things had now become somewhat serious, but I still didn't have any way to interrupt the proceedings.

'Help me get her legs apart.' Simon again. 'I want to have a look at it.'

My knees tried vainly to resist, but they were brushed unceremoniously aside.

'I love 'em,' said uncouth Simon. 'Female twats. The most gorgeous invention in the world. Look at that tender pink flesh hiding beneath the hair. Look at those lovely little crinkles. Doesn't it just turn you on?'

Fingers were pulling me apart, exposing me.

'Aesthetically I agree with you,' said Piers, 'but my

common sense tells me this could be construed as improper. We might find ourselves in a bit of trouble if we carry on.'

I was by now seriously disconcerted, but I had no means of expressing it. I couldn't even move. As I've said, my brain had become disassociated from my body. It was not me they were squeezing and tugging, but rather some inanimate object that was part of a biological experiment. I found my brain thinking as if it were an observer of this fascinating tableau, rather than the interested party. I recalled that much earlier, based on the discovery of some magazines hidden under my brother's bed, I had made the revolutionary deduction that men were in some incomprehensible way attracted to female breasts, the larger the better. I had learned that afternoon that bottoms also exercised this same inscrutable fascination. Now, surprise upon surprise, it appeared that these lads actually admired my little cavern as well. Odd, since it was something I had spent my life trying to hide. And the intriguing thing was that they had to be telling the truth. There was no point in their paying hollow compliments to an insensible girl. They really liked it.

But before I had time to come to terms with this unexpected revelation, I was shocked into consciousness by what happened next. A mouth – it couldn't possibly be anything else – attached itself to that part of me that I had previously only used to relieve my bladder, and began to suck and worry it with a fervour that the cream in any chocolate eclair would have been proud to induce. I gave one huge, involuntary shudder, and then, with a strange dizziness that I could not understand, my insides became flooded with a fluid I was hard put to identify.

'There you are, she loves it,' announced Simon proudly. 'Taste that!'

His mouth was replaced by another. More gentle this time, but ultimately just as invasive and demanding. I should be embarrassed, I thought. This is quite the most disgusting thing that's ever happened to me. Two men are taking it in turns to suck the juice from my passion fruit! Thank God I'm unconscious, otherwise I'd die of mortification.

'As sweet as pineapple,' confirmed Piers. 'I wish we could find a way of bottling it. We'd make a fortune.'

He was elbowed out the way and Simon's mouth returned with renewed energy to sample the waters. I'm losing my sanity, I thought, as I felt my insides respond to his urging. I realised that I was behaving both responsively and positively to their outrageous intimacy. Maybe I should become a prostitute when I get home, I thought. It might be fun.

'Let's just stick to this,' insisted Piers. 'No screwing. She might be a virgin, for all we know.'

Quite right, the real me commented.

'Are you crazy?' Simon practically exploded. 'I'm as hard as a British Rail sausage-roll. Besides, she's dying for it.'

'My turn,' said Piers. 'I want to roll her over. As she was on the beach.'

Two pairs of hands tugged me into the desired position, showing scant consideration for my sunburn.

'I really think that's the most beautiful bum I've ever seen,' said Piers, with true reverence in his voice. 'Let me put the flash on the camera. I've got to capture this on film.'

I heard him struggling frantically with Japanese technology while Simon got in a little bit of out-of-turn fondling, as he pulled and pushed at my yielding cheeks. My sunburn got a brief respite while the sound of clicking filled the room. I tried to shy away from the camera but my muscles were still not responding to instructions. What the hell had been in that cigarette?

'You know,' Piers continued thoughtfully, 'there is such a thing as true perfection in the female buttocks. Breasts aren't like that. They're all different. Some are big, some are small, and you can fancy both. But bums have to meet some strange ideal. This girl has an utterly perfect pair of globes. What's her name? Sarah? I'll put that on the photo.'

'Get on with it,' urged Simon. 'It's your turn. What are you going to do?'

'This,' said Piers. 'I thought of it on the beach and I've been longing to try it ever since.'

He lifted my hair and planted a gentle kiss on the nape of my neck.

That's not very original, I thought. Nice enough, but not very original. But I had underestimated him. With a long languid sweep his tongue ran down my neck, down my backbone, savouring its little bumps. Then it continued onwards, delving between my globes, onward and ever onward, caressing my tight, nervous anus, and then completing its journey at the door to paradise, which responded with yet another flood of welcoming melba sauce.

'I've never done that before,' Piers enthused.

'Did you...?' asked an admiring Simon.

'Yes,' Piers beamed.

'Blimey, I'm going to try it,' Simon vowed.

With that his hands pushed my buttocks apart.

'Take a photo of that,' he commanded. 'Before I kiss it.'

'Isn't it sweet? So tight,' said Piers, obliging. 'You know, I can't believe we lucked onto this peach.'

Simon's face burrowed into me and his tongue toyed with my most private orifice. I didn't believe it. Do men like anuses as well as breasts, twats, buttocks, and necks? What a terrifying world we live in! Is there no part of the female body they won't violate? But although I was genuinely appalled and embarrassed at the way I was being treated, I was also being mercilessly aroused. The Retsina had won. I gave another involuntary shudder, my stomach churned once again, and I could feel a thread of moisture actually running down the inside of my leg.

Then there was a loud hammering on the door and I heard Megan's voice calling out my name.

Bugger, I thought, wistfully. I'd been rescued in the nick of time.

# Chapter Three

Not surprisingly Peter and I received an extraordinary quantity of begging letters. I never saw any of them, of course. They were all handled by Peter's personal secretary, a woman called Jessica of indeterminate age yet unquestionable efficiency, who managed Peter's diary and indeed all of his time except when he was with me. One day, as a salutary exercise, Peter suggested that I go and talk to her about the pile of letters – several hundred of them – that were that one morning's intake.

'You cannot afford to take them seriously,' Jessica instructed me, 'otherwise you'd go mad.'

I picked one up and read it. The writer had apparently lost her husband in a car accident. One of her daughters had spina bifida, and another had trouble speaking and needed special remedial lessons. Her eldest, aged fourteen, she feared was already using hard drugs and was being coaxed into prostitution by her pusher. It was an incredible catalogue of woe. I looked at Jessica, appalled.

'Maybe it really is true,' I said in horror. 'Such things do happen.'

She looked at me patiently, and said, 'Oh yes, I don't doubt that many of these cases are highly deserving. But how could you possibly know which? And don't forget that everyone ultimately has recourse to welfare benefits. It's not generous but it's there. Perhaps this woman is telling the truth, but maybe she also spends all her dole money on ciggies and gin. You can be sure if you send her any money she'll be back for even more, and she'll probably tell her friends what a soft touch you are.'

I looked at the envelope.

'It was addressed to me, wasn't it?' I said. 'Not Peter.'

'Yes,' she said. 'You outscore him by about seven to one at the moment. But that's because his image is one of a hard-bitten businessman. In the public mind you're much more likely to give away your new-found wealth. Believe me, you don't even have time to read all this mail. I don't, I just sort it.'

I picked up a small brochure that was lying on top of the pile.

'But Peter and I don't even get to see circulars or advertisements,' I pointed out. 'How do you know we might not occasionally be interested?'

'I admit I have to make a snap decision,' she said. 'Many ads are from cranks, too. Just because that leaflet's professionally printed doesn't necessarily mean it's sane.' She picked up another one. 'Here, these people will send you a personal horoscope every month.'

I looked at the one I was holding. It was strangely mysterious; a picture of a beautiful old house on the cover, but no obvious indication of what it was selling. I looked inside. 'Athelstan Hall provides a unique and unusual service,' I read aloud. Oh yes, but what? 'Many young ladies lack self-confidence and fail to make the best use of their talents. Do you know someone whose personal relationships could benefit from Athelstan's intensive and unusual character-building environment?' It still wasn't clear what they were talking about. 'At Athelstan hall, in luxurious surroundings, your loved one will meet an encounter group she can confide in and learn from...'

I noticed Jessica was busy fishing around for other examples of outrageous literature, and I surreptitiously slipped the leaflet into my skirt pocket.

'Here!' she said triumphantly. 'The world will end on November twelfth next year. They've got proof! But can you explain to me why they sent their blurb to someone rich, instead of to the newspapers? Somewhere in the small-print they'll be asking for money, for sure.'

Somewhat subdued, I left her to her unenviable daily task. But back in my room I had a closer look at the Athelstan Hall leaflet. I understood that it offered weeklong residential courses specifically for young ladies, but it was oddly vague about the curriculum. Assertiveness, self-expression and expansiveness, were just a few of the attributes one might gain from an expensive stay within its walls. Correction was another curious term it used. It also persisted in addressing the man of the partnership, as if a woman could never be aware of her own inadequacies. I noticed that discrete sex therapy was mentioned. Was it run by a crank, or maybe a charlatan? I couldn't tell, but at the same time it seemed as though it could be remarkably apt for me in my current situation. It promised self-confidence. Well goodness, I was lacking in that! I experienced a shiver of curiosity. I couldn't go to a psychiatrist or marriage counsellor without seriously exposing Peter to unfair scrutiny. But I could go to a general-purpose encounter group, discuss real and imaginary hang-ups in an all-female circle, and perhaps chance upon some insight that could help me. There was even the possibility that there'd be someone there I could talk to who'd had difficulty losing her virginity but had finally succeeded. I knew I might be clutching at a straw, but it seemed I had little to lose. The cost was immaterial. In fact, the high price was somewhat comforting. You wouldn't be thrown in with any old Tom, Dick, or Harry.

It was, however, difficult to put the suggestion to Peter. I waited till after a heavy dinner and then fastened on to one of the leaflet's many promised offerings – social aptitude. I placed the brochure casually on the table.

'What would you think of me going on one of these women's assertiveness courses for a few days?' I gently probed. 'I still feel hopelessly inadequate when it comes to directing any of the staff, or hosting a dinner-party.'

'You've done pretty well so far,' he replied.

He glanced at the leaflet idly.

'Never heard of them,' he said dismissively. 'I could easily find you someone in the city who's job is imparting social graces, but I don't think you need it.'

'I don't want a crash course on flower-arranging or laying a dinner table,' I said. 'It's something much deeper than that. It's so easy for you; you've spent your whole life telling people what to do and they accept your direction happily. I can't even ask cook what we're having for supper without feeling I'm criticising her.'

Peter shrugged and smiled. 'Well of course I wouldn't stop you going if you wanted to,' he said. 'But I'm rather doubtful that they've got anything serious to offer.'

I left it at that, but a few days later, after what seemed like a whole day of telephone calls, Peter announced that he had to go to Tokyo on business. He had conceived the idea of adding a section of Japanese foods to each of his supermarkets and he wanted the products to be authentic. It was strange to see him actually excited about something.

'I'll be away for a week, I'm afraid,' he told me. 'Can you occupy yourself with the house and the garden?'

I pounced.

'I could do, but why don't I go to that assertiveness course I mentioned?' I suggested enthusiastically. 'That is, if they've got a place free at such short notice.'

'Sure, if you really want to,' he said. 'Get Jessica to ring them. But if you go and it turns out to be a complete farce don't be afraid to admit it. Just cut your losses and come home.'

It was of course time that drove Peter's life, not expense. A wasted day was irretrievable. A lost thousand pounds or two could easily be recouped. My time was nothing like so precious. I didn't expect any great revelations from the course itself, but I was prepared to give up a week's time in the hope I might stumble on some kindred spirit in the class who might directly or inadvertently help me to solve my increasingly serious problem with sex.

So the arrangements were duly made – at those prices I didn't really expect the establishment ever to admit it was full – and the following Sunday afternoon Peter drove me down to Sussex in the Aston Martin on his way to Gatwick for his overnight flight. A long tree-lined gravel drive took us to the imposing but not overbearing ivy-covered house of the picture, with huge mahogany front doors. Peter glanced agitatedly at his watch.

'I can't stop, I'm a little pressed for time,' he said, as he unloaded my cases. 'Ring the bell and tell them who you are. I'll phone you tomorrow evening, your time. I'll just be waking up for breakfast.' And with nothing more than a quick kiss he was gone.

It was strangely quiet. I half-expected to see groups of

sexually inadequate ladies wandering round the grounds in deep conversation, but there was no one. Just the birds singing in the trees and the gentle buzz of insects at the flowers in the warmth of the early evening. It was the first time I had been alone and in charge of my own destiny since getting married. I suddenly felt like a little girl again, terrified of the huge house and what it might contain. Everyone would be far more self-confident than me, I was sure.

But it had been my idea to come. I had burned my boats and now I had to make the best of it. I humped my cases over to the door, where there was a beautifully polished brass plate with the name *Athelstan Hall* on it.

Unfortunately someone had crudely tacked a piece of paper underneath.

*Sister Murdock's House of Correction*, it read.

I gasped. It was obviously an attempt at a joke by one of the guests, but for a new arrival it didn't bode too well. Did it perhaps mean that one was forced to eat nothing but salad and made to get up at six every morning for the good of one's soul? That's what I would have imagined a health farm would be like, though I had assumed this place was somewhat more subtle in its approach. I took a deep breath and tugged at the old-fashioned bell-pull. There was a distant jangling from somewhere within the building.

To my surprise a grey-haired nun opened the door.

'Hello, my dear,' she said. 'I'm Sister Murdock. Please come in.'

I struggled with the heavy cases.

'Goodness me,' she said. 'How embarrassing. We have no porter, I'm afraid. When someone as well known as you arrives I always feel so inadequate. Can you manage?'

I couldn't, but I did my best. Sister Murdock closed the front door behind me, and to my surprise locked it with a large iron key. My first impression was that the place was desperately old-fashioned. She opened the door of an office where a young woman with rimless glasses was busy at a computer.

'This is Katerina,' Sister Murdock said, 'our secretary, receptionist, and general factotum. Any administrative problems, you should see her. Katerina, this is Lady Sarah Easton.'

The woman leapt clumsily to her feet and actually curtsied to me. But she didn't offer to help me with my bags.

'I'll show you to your room, Lady Sarah,' said Sister Murdock.

She set off down one of the corridors and I struggled after her, cursing myself for having packed so many clothes. After all, I was only booked in for a five-night stay.

On the way we passed an open door. I stopped for a breather and a peek inside. It was a gym, with various bits of equipment including training bicycles, exercise machines and the like. The place was a physical fitness centre, I decided. But then, bizarrely, I noticed that in one corner was a bucking bronco thing; one of those fairground machines you have to ride as long as you can until it throws you off. I was intrigued. Perhaps someone had a sense of humour, after all.

Sister Murdock was now halfway up the staircase and I had to hurry after her, suffering badly from having worn my grey suit with the tight skirt. It rode up hopelessly as I struggled up the stairs, and the larger of the two cases managed to ladder my stocking. Being Lady Sarah had made me perpetually self-conscious, half-believing that the paparazzi were round every corner waiting to snap me in compromising circumstances. Now, feeling like a little girl, I glanced nervously over my shoulder, but the place was still deserted. No one to watch my discomfort, thank heavens.

My room, when I finally reached it, was small but comfortably furnished. I set down the cases with a gasp and went over to the window. The view was superb; a charming old garden with holly-hocks and delphiniums in front, and trees behind, against a tall moss-covered wall further in the distance. Then I noticed with something of a shock that there were bars on the outside of the window. To be sure they were tastefully fashioned wrought iron, but bars, nevertheless. It reinforced the fear I had felt outside; that I was entering an enclosed world in which I would be found woefully inadequate. But I was determined to at least appear sophisticated. I nodded towards the bars with raised eyebrows.

'Ah yes,' said Sister Murdock. 'I regret that some of our visitors, particularly those who have come here because of drug problems or whatever, sometimes have to be restrained from trying to climb out. Pay no attention.'

I'd had no idea, of course, that people went there for such extreme reasons.

But I supposed she was right. It was a dangerous drop outside, being from the second floor. Perhaps that also explained the locked front door. I've heard that people on a cold turkey cure can get pretty desperate.

'Dinner is at six o'clock sharp,' she went on. 'You have plenty of time. There's a toilet and washbasin in here,' she said, opening a door into a room little bigger than a cupboard, 'but if you want a shower I'm afraid you have to walk down to the end of the landing. After you've freshened up go back down the stairs the way we came, to the front door, and then just beyond that is the dining room.

'Six o'clock,' she repeated.

I glanced at my watch and decided it would be worth the effort to have a shower. After all, these institution meals never start right on the dot. I found the bathroom where she had indicated, but was amazed to see that the showers were not in individual cubicles as any civilised person would expect, but all together in an open area, just like an old school or sports pavilion. I cursed myself under my breath. I was really slumming it here. And for why? I should have stayed at home. Had I voluntarily consigned myself to an ancient Victorian workhouse, where they fed us on gruel and made us run ten miles a day? I groaned under my breath, but then glanced nervously at my watch. Suddenly, in the draught from an open window, I felt as though I was back at school. Perhaps it would be better to get to dinner on time after all.

I dried myself and dressed hurriedly – my Janet Passim jersey and a simple pair of maroon Lacoste jogging trousers – and set off downstairs. I was feeling distinctly lonely. Where was everyone? I was terrified of having to make a decent impression on the strangers I would meet, but I was even more scared of finding no one at all, like a ghost house. Then I heard a murmur of voices and found the dining room by following it.

When I walked in the door I got quite a shock. There were only seven other guests, but they were already eating their soup. Their eyes looked up to meet mine and I caught recognition in most of them. But there was no one to greet me and I had to take my place on the end of the bench at a long wooden table. It resembled nothing more than a monk's refectory. There wasn't even a tablecloth. As soon as I had sat down a mousy little waitress hurried up and gave me a plate of soup with a strange little nod that seemed to say she was doing me a dangerous favour; feeding me after the bell, so to speak.

I took a deep breath, aggrieved that nobody had spoken to me.

'Hello, I'm Sarah Easton,' I said, holding out my hand to the girl I had sat next to.

'I'm Astrud,' she said. 'Astrud Peterson. I run an employment agency in real life. Welcome to Hell Hall.'

As she said that I noticed that one of the other girls gave her a severe glance as if to warn her to keep her mouth shut. I realised that all of us were about the same age, certainly no one over thirty. In fact, my fellow guests formed a strangely striking group. There was an imposing black girl who towered over the others, even sitting down. Another self-effacing but still eye-catching Asian had hair that reached below the bench she was sitting on. There was also a brash redhead who looked vaguely familiar – as if she could be in show business. Astrud herself was remarkable for her soft, generous looks, while she sat next to another tall girl who introduced herself as Freya. She had large convex glasses that made her look fierce and domineering. I felt nervous in the others' presence, aware that I might be the youngest there. But I also felt a flicker of hope. No, these weren't ordinary people, in fact one or two looked very intense. Conversation certainly seemed unlikely to be dull. Good.

'Is this all there are of us?' I asked Astrud.

'I guess so,' she replied. 'I must say, I was expecting more. Would you like some wine?'

I smiled gratefully and nodded. Based on what I'd seen so far I'd been prepared for the place to be teetotal. 'Is it real?' I asked.

'I should say so,' she said.

I sipped gingerly at the white wine she had poured from a simple carafe, and was inordinately pleased to discover it was delicious. From the Perigord region, I would have guessed, based on my experience of eating out with Peter. Well, at least I wasn't at the mercy of a self-denial fanatic. I finished my glass in a couple of gulps and refilled it quickly, while there was still plenty left.

'Hello, my name's Millicent,' said the smartly dressed, dark-haired girl opposite me. 'This was my husband's idea. I've no idea what we're in for, but apparently SM is going to give us a little introductory speech after we've eaten.'

'SM?' I asked.

'Sister Murdock, silly,' she informed me.

Just like me, all these girls seemed to have noticed there was something vaguely forbidding about the set-up, although it was difficult to put a finger on what it was. One could not fault the dinner. The soup, a very palatable concoction of leek and watercress, was followed by a tasty stifado of pork, beef and paprika, with crusty bread – no potatoes – and as a finale we were treated to one of the best Cerises Flambe au Kirsch I have ever tasted. It was all served by the self-effacing waitress who seemed to speak only when under duress. An abstainer's diet this was not, but that was surely a relief. I hadn't come to get slim.

When I'd polished off the last of the Kirsch sauce I realised I was beginning to feel the effects of the alcohol combined with the extra tension brought on by the situation. The carafe up our end of the table had been readily refilled and I had appropriated far more than my fair share.

There was a sharp hand-clap and I looked up to see Sister Murdock standing at the head of the table.

'Good evening, ladies, and welcome to a new week at Athelstan Hall,' she welcomed us.

There was a cautious murmur of response from the table.

'None of you have been here before, I see, so you cannot know what to expect,' she went on. 'A couple of you have come voluntarily, which is excellent. But the rest of you have probably been lured here under some form of false pretences. No matter; you're probably the ones most likely to benefit from your stay.

'We are not, I must emphasise, a health or beauty clinic designed, as so many of them are, to minister to the body or external appearance. We deal in minds. You've all heard, I am sure, of outward-bound schools. These are admirable institutions where managers or jaded executives are sent to participate, sometimes against their will, in a variety of arduous physical tasks, such as camping out overnight in appalling weather. Not a pleasant experience while it's happening, but one that almost invariably broadens the horizon, breeds team spirit, and puts stultified brains back in gear.

'I want you to think of Athelstan Hall in much the same light. Each and every one of you will be lacking in some facet of your psychological make-up. No one but a fool is ever completely satisfied with their capabilities. You're all young ladies. Are you assertive enough in your public or private lives? Can you deal with a serious crisis? This week we shall find out. Your husbands or families may have made the decision to send you here, in which case they will have already passed on their reasons to me. Maybe you have come to rely too heavily on drink. Maybe you are a designer and your innovative spark has disappeared. Maybe you have been unfaithful to your spouse. Mending such mental lesions can never be painless, and like the overweight executive forced to run ten miles at an outward-bound school, you must expect to suffer, at least mentally. Indeed, I assure you that you *will* suffer. But I am confident you will also strengthen your minds and characters.'

She paused ominously. I felt justified in leaping to my feet and saying that her brochure had never hinted that we were in for that tough a time, but of course I was far too self-conscious to do so.

'You should understand,' she continued, 'that we deal in truth here. So much of our lives is wasted in some sham. At Athelstan truth is king. You will each be expected to undergo a strenuous interrogation by the others. You can fight the truth, of course – we all do – but you will benefit if you let it out. You must learn to submit to the group, both physically and mentally. One of the most valuable assets of a young lady is to be able to accept subjugation willingly. It's also one of the hardest to attain, to enjoy domination for its own sake. If that sounds ominous let me qualify the threat by saying that like outward-bound we have no wish to harm any of you. We have to push you till you bend. But we shall not push you till you break.

'Now, the first of our little games. One of the house rules is that we impose a forfeit on the last to sit down for dinner every evening. Tonight, your first night, this will be little more than a token penalty. However, you must expect this to increase in severity as the week passes. We won't build your characters by making you recite some poem backwards, will we? No, your tribulation needs to be a lot more severe than that. Would you all look over there, above the fireplace, please?'

We turned, dutifully. Over the mantelpiece hung a strange wooden object with the shape of a flat spade, but slightly curved like a miniature hockey stick. On it were some delicate carvings which made it a very satisfying *objet d'art*. But surely it was more than just an ornament.

'That is from South America,' Sister Murdock went on. 'It's made from a very light but hard wood, and it was originally used to paddle a canoe. But we have a different purpose in mind for it. That is our equivalent of a cane, although I assure you it's a great deal less barbaric. It stings but does not cut. In the morning the last to arrive for breakfast will have to show the courage to accept chastisement with that.'

I was having difficulty believing my ears. This was positively Victorian!

She couldn't go around beating her paying guests! Could she? I waited for one of the others to object, but no one did. I began to suffer severe qualms.

They all seemed to have accepted that they were in for a grim time. Perhaps they even believed it was legitimate to chastise one's guests, if one claimed it was to strengthen their character!

Sister Murdock continued.

'Tonight you may complain that you had no warning of the impending forfeit. That is true, of course, although I expressly asked each of you to be here at six, sharp. Let me see. We have a well known face amongst us this week. Lady Sarah Easton, would you stand up please?'

I rose to my feet unsteadily, too cautious of all those unfamiliar faces to make a fuss.

'Millicent Andrews, a talented photographer from North London, was the next to last to arrive,' the woman announced. 'Would you stand up too, please?'

Millicent got to her feet and gave me a nervous, conspiratorial grin.

'It would be unkind to be too harsh on you both, on your first evening,' acknowledged Sister Murdock. 'So I think instead I will impose a simple competition. You will take it in turns to drink a glass of wine, until one of you gives in.'

A mild forfeit? Not for me. I was more than a little taken aback at the thought of such a contest. The extraordinary truth of the situation was that I had not allowed myself to get seriously drunk ever since those shameful events on Lindos, three years earlier. And I really wanted my wits about me this evening. I was acutely conscious of my image as Lady Sarah Easton. That would be hard to maintain if I was dizzy with drink. Never mind, I thought, I'd fake it. I'd throw in the sponge after two glasses. Admit defeat like a lady.

But it wasn't that easy. Millicent drank the first glass, slowly and with an enormous flourish. There was an infectious cheer from around the table. I could not cave in without a fight, or I'd look as though I was acting high-and-mighty. Instead, I drained my first glass in one spectacular gulp, and was relieved to hear a similar cheer. Suddenly I wanted the other girls to be on my side. Coming into the hall last had set me strangely apart from them.

Millicent finished her second, but less than impressively. A stream of wine ran from the side of her mouth and down onto her shirt. The absent-minded way she kept dabbing ineffectually at it convinced me that she was already not totally in control of her actions. Perhaps I could win without sinking too far into the morass of drunkenness. I drank, not quickly this time, but still steadily. Another cheer went up and I attempted a gracious smile.

Millicent looked distinctly green as she struggled with her third, but to my frustration she finished it. I'd resolved not to go beyond two, but a boxer can't throw the fight when he's obviously winning. I sank my third and then grimaced. That strange, distant feeling had suddenly flooded over me. This was wicked stuff. German Liebfraumilch is often only eight percent proof. The best French vintages can be twelve or thirteen percent. We were definitely with one of the best.

I was sure Millicent would now capitulate, but with dogged determination she forced the fourth down, bit by bit. She held her glass triumphantly upside-down, and then it promptly slipped from her fingers and crashed on the floor. I decided I was all done. I would drink the next glass down to about halfway, and then collapse back onto the bench. But the other girls set up a chant, 'More, more, more…' It reminded me vaguely of being back at boarding-school, playing hockey or something. A crowd is heady medicine, even if it's only seven strong. Before I knew where I was the glass was almost empty. I caught sight of Milly's face, red and sweaty, dreading the next glass, and I knew I must look the same way. Deliberately I fell back and theatrically plunged my head into my arms.

There was a chorus of booing. Astrud nudged me fiercely. 'It's only a teaspoonful,' she hissed.

She was right. How could I chicken out now? I picked up the glass, which really did not contain more than a thimbleful, threw my head back and swallowed that last little drop. At the moment I did it seemed easy, but directly I put the glass down I knew I'd gone too far. The room was swaying and the din from the crowd, though no less noisy, had receded strangely into the distance.

Of course Millicent must now give in. But she didn't! I couldn't believe it. To a din of encouragement she sipped her next glass a teaspoonful at a time, and miraculously it all disappeared. How could she have done it? And on top of whatever she'd drunk during the meal! Or had she been drinking water? Anyway, it was over. My reluctance was no longer faked. I managed less than a quarter of the glass before I gave up for good. No amount of encouragement would change that.

'I can't drink another drop,' I sobbed, surprised to find the tears weren't forced.

I was suddenly in a very emotional state, brought on by the uncertainty engendered by Athelstan Hall, by my ever-present disappointment in bed with Peter, and by what must have been in all eight or nine glasses – well over a bottle – of a very potent wine.

'Well done, both of you,' said Sister Murdock, magnanimously. 'Sarah, you are clearly the loser. Would you stand on the table, please?'

So the old bitch wasn't done with me yet. I got grimly to my feet and climbed unsteadily up onto the wooden table, with lots of pushing and steadying from the other girls. Through my dizziness it did occur to me that Sister Murdock's bullying had already had an effect. We felt like a group – us against her. I was already part of that group, possibly even its temporary leader, since I had suffered the most. So she was certainly no fool. But any temporary admiration I felt soon disappeared as it became clear how extreme her ideas were.

'One of the more difficult accomplishments I want you all to learn while you are here is that of being able to release yourself from your inhibitions at the appropriate time,' she announced. 'Submission, as I said, is the key to a fulfilling life. It's not easy, as poor Lady Sarah, now standing exposed on that table will undoubtedly learn. I have here a recording I should like you all to listen to. The point of this exercise is that you should consciously try to enjoy hearing these sounds.'

And with that she turned on a tape player and stepped back, leaving us all to listen. For a time my ears remained out of tune and unable to assimilate anything, but then I began to discern some tiny, sporadic whimpers, like the suppressed crying of a scolded child. The noise grew in volume and then gradually in intensity till at last, with a shock, I realised it was not a child at all but a woman. And the noises she was making were clearly sexual in nature.

From my elevated position I glanced down, and could tell that some but not all the girls had grasped the recording's content. The sound was physically embarrassing, recalling immediately all of the most undesirable aspects of sexism; female subjugation, male urgency, and worst of all, unconditional female gratitude.

I could imagine the girl writhing and begging shamelessly for the man to overwhelm her. My body felt hot and flushed all over, and the only thing I could think of was that I wanted the sounds to stop. Once again, as I had before the wedding, I cursed my own virginal status. The girls would look up at me, I was sure, and guess my guilty secret, now a hundred times more mortifying since I was a married woman. I glanced away at Sister Murdock and found that she was indeed staring very pointedly at me, as if assessing my reaction.

Soon the whole dining hall was filled with the obscene noise and everyone present could no longer have any doubt as to what they were listening to; the clandestine recording of some poor girl who was being loved almost beyond endurance, and who had no idea that her surrender would be used later as an object lesson to a public class. It was disgraceful, in my opinion.

At last, when I had almost got to the point of jumping off the table and running from the room, Sister Murdock hit the stop button and a merciful silence engulfed us.

'So there it is,' she said. 'Now I know what you're all thinking – that the girl was recorded without her knowledge. But that is not so. That was a past student at one of these courses and she allowed the recorder to be present while she made love. A brave girl and an extremely self-confident one, I think you'll agree. How many of you could do that, I wonder?'

How many would want to? was what I would have liked to shout at her. Her ideas were downright crazy! Certain sounds should, in my opinion, only be heard in privacy and by those whose actions cause them. But once more I lacked the nerve – Sister Murdock would probably have said the self-confidence – to make a fuss.

'Right,' she continued. 'We have introduced the ugly subject of sex. I must confess I am an ardent student of Freud, and he believed that most human hang-ups had their root cause in some sort of sexual insecurity. I have no idea how each of you individually feels about sex, but I'm willing to bet that between you there's a skeleton or two in the cupboard. This week we're going to dig those skeletons out, I'm afraid. I said things wouldn't be easy.'

At this point, although drunk, I became very apprehensive indeed. I had imagined an encounter group would act as an umbrella whereby one could discuss problems almost as if they pertained to someone else. In some quiet corner I had hoped to be able to laughingly disclose my concerns to a sympathetic but private ear. But I could already see that Sister Murdock would have other ideas. She would not be happy until we were all bleeding in public, and that was the last thing I wanted to do. I forced myself to concentrate on what she was saying.

'We now come to the point of the evening where we introduce a little humour. If this were a male stag party I am sure it would be time to tell some smutty jokes. But we shall be just a little more subtle, but the subject – sex – will be the same. Throughout my speech I have referred continuously to "we", as the staff of Athelstan. But so far you have seen only Mandy, our cook and waitress, and me. So now look around and you will see "them".'

There was an extraordinary shriek from one of the guests beside me, and then we all joined in the girlish screaming. I threw my hands over my face in a gesture of disbelief, but when I peeked between my fingers they were still there. In the four corners of the room, having crept in without us hearing them, were four men, now standing impassively. Each of them was dressed very smartly in immaculate black tie and dinner-suit... but each also wore a heavy and unbelievably bizarre mask! One wore a bird's head, one a frog, one a bull, and the last a red dragon!

Sister Murdock drew our attention again. It was only at that point that I reminded myself that she was a nun. What could she be thinking of? In fact, what was this whole silly fiasco in aid of? I was a respectable public figure. How could I be now standing on a table, surrounded by ridiculously masked men? Was it a dream? Had I assigned myself to a lunatic asylum? Would someone please take me home?

'I should like to acquaint you with our male friends,' the woman went on. 'They are a cosmopolitan crowd – no two of them from the same country. The names I have chosen for them are as follows: the one with the bald eagle's head is Rod. Our handsome dragon is Lance, that ugly-looking frog is Pearce, and last but by no means least, the bull is Spike.'

The nervous giggling continued, though the men moved not at all, standing like statues in their respective corners. Sister Murdock called for silence again.

'Our friends have two roles to play in your week here at Athelstan,' she announced. 'I must now reveal to you that your plight is far more serious than you may have imagined.

'None of you is able to leave the house. The doors are locked, the windows are barred. Should you attempt to escape, Rod, Lance, Pearce or Spike will bring you back, and you may be sure your mischief will not go unpunished.

'Ritual is a very important aspect of an establishment

like Athelstan Hall; the ritual punishment for the last arrival at dinner, the ritual selection of one of you for the day's truth session. Our four men are part of that ritual, too. While they are on duty they become your slaves. You are all paying heavily for the privilege of staying here. You would expect some service, I think. Someone to post your letters, perhaps, or to shine your shoes or brush your hair. These chores they will perform without complaint, together indeed, with anything else you may care to ask of them. They are, quite literally, at your beck and call. And you will find that being in total control of another human is in itself a difficult and mind-broadening experience. Suffice it to say, they have been instructed to obey your every wish.'

I was swaying unsteadily as the wine took an ever-deeper grip on my brain. This was no bloody nun, I thought. She was some sort of freak, an aged and frustrated sexual libertine. She should have been wearing a dirty raincoat.

Unfortunately that kinkiness made her all the more dangerous. A prisoner? Well, we'd soon see about that. It's illegal to hold someone against their will. Just as soon as I'd had a night's rest I would get on to Peter's solicitor and have the whole place closed down.

'Quiet, please,' said Sister Murdock, wearily. 'We have just one more little ritual before you're all free to go to your rooms. Sarah's forfeit. She's been a good sport, I'm sure you'll agree. Now let's see if she can succeed in one last test.' She waved towards the silent men. 'All completely immobile, aren't they? The trousers tailored perfectly flat at the front.

'Sarah,' she looked up at me, 'your task, while still standing on this table, is to distend those crisply tailored trousers. Can you do that, I wonder? I rather hope so.'

Now there was silence, with everyone looking at me expectantly. This was preposterous! Stuff your bloody forfeit, was what I wanted to say. But the other girls clearly expected me to oblige. Excitement sparkled in their eyes and Astrud gave me a conspiratorial wink. I couldn't refuse. Miss high-and-mighty they would dub me for sure – a poor sport, a party-pooper. I would have my confrontation with Sister Murdock all in good time, and then I would win. But not in front of all the girls. I had to believe I could make them my friends and allies.

Hardly knowing what I was doing, I found myself pulling the expensive sweater up and over my head. I twirled it round three times and then threw it away towards the fireplace, where mercifully it missed the grate itself. The men remained impassive. I wriggled out of my jogging trousers, throwing them in the opposite direction. The girls had started another chant to encourage me but I noted, as I tottered on legs that felt like bits of string, that so far my exertions had had no effect. Anger welled up inside me. I was beautiful, dammit! Why weren't these men overcome by my charms? I took rapid stock of the situation. If I went on like this I'd quickly be nude, and worse, my objective might still be unattained. How humiliating! I would have to dance smarter, not faster.

I closed my eyes, raised my arms above my head, and began to writhe. I've never been a particularly good dancer, but the movements I was called upon to perform were so basic they came more or less naturally. Lots of hip, buttock, and chest. At last I heard a suppressed clearing of a throat and I permitted myself a squint through half-closed eyes. The dragon was yielding to my begging, and so was the frog. Their trousers had begun to form into embarrassing tents. But there was still a long way to go.

I knew the girls were expecting me to take my bra off. It was the obvious next step, but one so obvious that I was determined not to do it. I thought back to my days on the beach at Lindos. 'Your bum is your fortune,' Megan had said. She had been proved right then, perhaps she could be again.

I reached down and took hold of my panties, pulling them upwards very slowly. The front soon formed a fierce V; white cotton against the marzipan tan I had acquired in St Kitts. Ever tighter I pulled it, till it was nothing more than a narrow thong between my two bronzed cheeks. I rotated, presenting my rear to the men one at a time, writhing and thrusting, beckoning, wheedling. I wanted them to want me, to long for my body.

The girls had all gone silent now, fascinated by the tension in the air, watching the men, willing them to succumb. I had realised that the initial spur is the most difficult. Once the blood had started flowing there was little they could do to hold themselves back, except possibly to shut their eyes, and my magnetism was a little too strong to permit that. The first two, Lance and Pearce, were mine, stiff as ramrods, pointing skywards. Rod hung grimly back at first, but then his resistance broke and pretty soon his trousers bulged impressively.

Spike was the last to respond, but with three down and only one to concentrate on I knew he was mine. My globes glowered at him, promising paradise. Come inside, they begged, drawing the eye down to my crotch. I could hear his hoarse breathing from inside the bull's head and then, like a pointer identifying the prey, his trousers grew an incriminating nose. Four helpless pikestaffs now stood to attention, their owners my slaves.

Mission accomplished, I gave a quick bow, clambered unsteadily from the table, and ran to my room, weeping with emotion and exhaustion.

# Chapter Four

Once in the privacy of my room I fell sobbing on the bed. What a slut I was!

Fancy cavorting in front of an audience like that! Peter would be appalled. I simply had to remember that my life was no longer my own. I visualised a photograph of me, lasciviously drunk and prancing on a table, appearing in next week's *Sunday Globe*. That would be the end of our marriage.

I would say that I was forced into doing it, but no one would believe me for a moment. Besides, it was obviously untrue. I had enjoyed doing it, however indignant I pretended to be. The simple truth was that I was proud of my obscene display.

I had dominated the emotions of four men just by dancing for them. My reward had been their unmistakable arousal. All of them had involuntarily revealed that they wanted me. I had been a slut in Lindos. I was still a slut now, despite being a virgin.

Abruptly I buried my face in my hands again, even though there was no one else present. I had just imagined the most vivid tableau; myself, nude on the wooden table, the four men still wearing their masks, making the most violent use of my body while the girls looked on, cheering.

It was so disgusting!

But what was more disgusting than the vision was the warm feeling of excitement and longing it generated in me. If only I wasn't Lady Sarah. If only I could, just for once, rut like a bitch on heat, feeling four pairs of hands running over my body, enjoying their touch instead of shying away from it.

That was the significance of the masks, after all. One could forget for an hour or two one's upbringing and the conventions of proper behaviour, and simply be someone else.

Just then there was a cautious knock on my bedroom door. I sat up quickly on the bed and wiped the tearstains from my face.

'Who is it?' I called.

'It's Mandy,' came the reply. 'Lady Sarah, can I talk to you, please?'

I didn't recognise the voice but I could not fail to detect the strength of the entreaty. I opened the door. It was the tiny little pixie who had served us dinner. I beckoned her inside and we sat on the bed.

'I recognised you at once,' she said. 'I can't begin to say how much I admire you. You're everything I would want to be – tall, self-possessed, utterly lovely. I've come to ask you an enormous favour.'

I tried not to groan. She wanted my bloody autograph for her child. But I was wrong, so wrong.

'You know Rod, the one with the eagle's head?' she said.

'Only from the neck down,' I replied sourly.

'He's a real dish, in my opinion,' she said, eyes sparkling. 'He's promised to come to my room tonight. He's not supposed to because I'm only one of the staff, but I persuaded him to be kind to me.'

I was immediately embarrassed that this girl, a complete

stranger, should be talking to me about her sexual liaisons.

'So?' I replied shortly.

I was really puzzled. I couldn't imagine a stud like Rod seeing anything worth having in my new acquaintance. Her ears stuck out like wing-mirrors, and her whole face was strangely pointed, like a squirrel's. And her hard little chest had less shape than a boy's. Surely he'd be better off making love to a French loaf.

'I don't quite know how to put this, Lady Sarah,' she went on, and then paused. 'I know from past experience that it may not work.'

'I don't think I understand,' I said, really wanting to be left alone.

'Well, he won't be able to get it up,' she said sheepishly. 'It's me, of course. I've got about as much sex appeal as a pillar-box in the rain. He certainly wouldn't have agreed to come tonight except that you turned him on. I could see he was desperate after you'd left – his erection wouldn't go away. He was dreaming of having you, although of course he knew he couldn't. So I took him aside and told him he could get it from me instead.'

Although a few seconds earlier I had been fantasising about being taken by all four men, I was now angry that Rod should imagine satisfying himself with my body and that Mandy should see herself as a surrogate for me.

'The best of luck to you, then, Mandy,' I said coldly.

'No, no, I *know* he'll fail,' she persisted. 'Wouldn't you, in his position? He'll get up to my room, randy as a teapot with two spouts, and then the moment he sees me he'll wobble. And I'll have to spend another bloody night biting the sheets.'

All at once I felt sorry for her. What an appalling plight!

Just because she was as ugly as a slice of half-eaten toast in a waste-bin didn't mean her feelings weren't just as strong as any other woman's. Stronger, no doubt, since she must rarely, if ever, get satisfactorily plonked.

'But there's nothing I can do,' I said, more sympathetically.

'Yes there is,' she insisted. 'You could be there.'

'What on earth for?' As usual, with anything to do with sex, I was slow off the mark.

'He can look at you while he bonks me,' she declared.

I was stunned. 'Mandy, that's preposterous!' I exclaimed.

'Please!' she pleaded. 'Can't you see how much this means to me? I'm thirty-two, and with my plain looks that means I'm well past my sell-by date. This is my one and only chance to get humped by a real man, instead of some creep who's so drunk he doesn't know what he's doing.'

'I can't possibly do what you're asking!' I said. 'Suppose the story got into the papers? Suppose my husband heard about it? Suppose Rod turns out to be a blackmailer?'

She hesitated, taken aback by an argument she'd never even considered.

'I know!' she said enthusiastically, 'you can wear his mask. It's only your body he needs to see, Lady Sarah. I'll let him in in the dark. Then we can shine the bedside lamp on you, when you're incognito.'

'He'd be bound to guess it was me,' I protested.

'Doesn't matter,' she said excitedly. 'He couldn't prove it. That's the point.'

'No, no, it's quite ridiculous.' But as I shook my head I once again felt that flood of erotic excitement. The image was compulsive; a spotlight directed at my provocative body while a drooling, gasping man emptied himself into this eager receptacle.

'I can only beg,' said Mandy. 'It's within your power to give me one perfect memory to take to my old age. That's all I ask.'

I must refuse, of course. Unless I could justify my actions through expediency... surely the waitress couldn't be locked up as well as the guests.

Wouldn't it be nice to outwit Sister Murdock?

'Can you get me out of here?' I bargained. 'Tomorrow morning?'

Mandy gasped. 'We're not supposed to—'

'Come on,' I urged. 'You said this was your once-in-a-lifetime opportunity. Surely you'll break a few rules for that.'

She looked at me earnestly, and then nodded and said, 'I have to go into town tomorrow. In the car...'

'Right,' I said determinedly. 'Then I'll do what you want.'

Mandy got to her feet eagerly. 'Marvellous!' she squeaked.

'Just a minute,' I said, interrupting her joy. I slipped quickly out of my underwear and put on one of the three dressing gowns I'd brought; red silk, with a corded belt.

We hurried furtively down the corridor and then, to my surprise, up yet another staircase to somewhere in the attic area. Mandy's room was tiny. If you attempted to open one of the cupboard drawers it would get in bed with you.

'When's he coming?' I asked in a conspiratorial whisper. The frantic scamper through corridors and up the stairs had taken me back to my schooldays at Westover. It was as if we were playing a prank on one of the other girls.

Mandy glanced at her watch. 'He said around eleven. We've got a few minutes. Let's get things set up.'

She directed me to stand at the side of the bed, pointing the primitive bedside lamp at me so that my head was in shadow, but my dressing gown was illuminated from neck to knees. Then she switched off the main light.

'How will that look?' she asked.

I realised I was expected to take the gown off. Feeling like a mischievous teenager I did so. But I was shaken abruptly out of my schoolgirl reverie by the tableau I presented. The lamp shone harshly on my breasts, throwing them into startling relief. Even my navel stood out, black and bottomless against the gentle swell of my belly.

Below that the normally sedate tangle of hair seemed to leap forward in a tawny mass, before my thighs plunged into the shadows. Good grief, I was even turning myself on! I glanced up to see Mandy's dimly lit eyes staring at me in awe.

'Even your hair colour's natural, isn't it?' she whispered.

The bitterness in her voice left me no answer worth saying. She undressed too, and I had to prevent myself from glancing away self-consciously. I've likened her body to a stick of French bread, and that describes the upper half very well. She had absolutely nothing on her chest except a couple of spots that could well have been pustules, for all the shape they had. Below the waist, however, she suddenly swelled out, with a very prominent bottom, so that in total she resembled an under-ripe pear. I began to appreciate that I should not regard my own looks as merely a lucky endowment, but rather as something precious for which I should be infinitely grateful.

'Can you do me one more favour?' she asked.

She pulled the heavy cord out from my dressing gown and handed it to me.

'Beat me with that,' was her amazing request. 'Just on the bottom.'

'What on earth for?' I gasped.

'To make the skin pink and bruised. It'll turn him on. My bum's the only thing I've got with any sex appeal so I have to make best use of it.'

She climbed onto the bed and crouched on her knees and elbows so that her bottom was higher than her head. It registered on me that her globes were actually very well shaped, tight and perky, with a deep inviting cleavage. I was well past the stage of asking questions, so I did what she wanted, striking her three or four times.

'Much harder than that,' she urged.

I swung again.

'Harder,' she urged again. 'It's got to tingle, otherwise it's no good.'

I lashed out viciously with the rope and she gasped with pain.

'That's good,' she sighed. 'Just a couple more times.'

I folded the cord double and swung with all my might. Her body lurched forward under the attack. She grunted and bit her lip, but forced herself back into the same submissive position. I'd never beaten anyone before. Why was it her buttocks looked so inviting?

'One more, and that's all.' It was actually herself she was reassuring. The flesh was already striped red and angry. I lashed out joyfully again and she clenched desperately at the side of the bed, holding back a cry.

'Thank you... Lady Sarah...' she managed.

'Call me Sally,' I said. 'Are you all right?' I was beginning to admire the girl's strength of character. She resembled a plucky little pixie with the courage of a giant.

'Yes, thank you, Sally. It's only a silk rope, after all. No doubt you'll see plenty more beatings before your week's out.'

It was an extraordinary remark to make, all the more so because it was said so casually. It was as if Athelstan Hall was some sort of a punishment dungeon, and everyone knew it but me. A chastisement centre. I'd heard that some people willingly submitted themselves to such treatment, as a strange thrill. I hoped people did not think that of me.

There were footsteps on the stairs outside. I quickly turned the lamp off so that we were in total darkness.

'Come in,' said Mandy, as he knocked on the door.

He was silhouetted in the doorway, still wearing the eagle mask.

'Don't turn on the light,' said Mandy, hurriedly. 'Give me your mask.'

He obeyed without asking the reason. She handed it to me in the darkness and I slipped it over my head. Rod's face, I meanwhile observed, was quite as handsome as his body, with a crowning mop of curls made hopelessly untidy by the prolonged spell inside the mask. Then he shut the door and we were once more cloaked in blackness.

'I've a treat for you, Rod,' Mandy said.

She turned on the bedside lamp, and for a moment the only thing visible in the room was my body, its voluptuousness exaggerated by the shadows. Rod gasped and I saw him reach towards me.

Mandy pushed his hand away. 'No, no,' she halted his

advance. 'Don't touch. You can only look.'

His hesitation spoke volumes. Why should I screw this stick insect, it said, when I could have the damselfly instead. But the logic of the situation was clear. The stick was available, the damsel was not.

To my surprise, instead of indulging in any normal foreplay, Mandy resumed her inelegant but submissive posture on the bed, head against the coverlet and bottom thrust out, inviting penetration. With his jaw hanging partway open and his eyes fixed avidly on my bosom Rod began fumbling with his clothes, removing them hastily. I was proud to observe that his spear was already fiercely rampant. Hidden behind my mask I was able to observe it unashamedly.

I realised that this was the first time that such an opportunity for leisurely observation had offered itself, and I resolved to make best use of it. It was a handsome device, firm and straight, and its head poked out from under the covers like some eager one-eyed mole, determined to burrow its way into any dark cavern it could find. But it was clear that determination was not enough. Rod grunted and Mandy squealed, but entrance was not forthcoming.

'Hold it just a minute,' said Rod. As if it were all part of a day's work, his face disappeared behind her buttocks with only his eyes peering over the swell, still riveted on my treasures.

'What have you done to yourself, honey?' he asked suddenly. 'Your bottom's all bruised.'

'I thought you'd like it,' Mandy said, her voice muffled by the coverlet. 'I wanted to suffer for you.'

'I *do* like it,' he rasped. 'It's so hot and tender.'

For a while he smothered her buttocks with kisses, occasionally forgetting to stare at me. Mandy sighed happily, and looking up at me from her cramped position she whispered, 'It was worth it.' She reached out and took my hands in hers so that I became an accomplice to her enjoyment. Rod finished his tour of the twin domes, burying his face between them, licking and worrying till he believed he had achieved the desired result. Then he stood up and blew me a kiss before once again grasping his member with his right hand while guiding it home with his left.

The precise moment when he invaded her body was obvious. Mandy gave a gasp and a sharp intake a breath, and her hands gripped mine urgently. Rod grunted with the effort but gave a short release of air as he achieved his objective.

'Jesus, that's tight,' he muttered, the strain showing on his face.

He worked away cautiously for some minutes, but then things seemed to free themselves as Mandy became more relaxed. A look of businesslike determination shone in his eyes, a true professional encountering a tricky pitch but taking all difficulties in his stride. Mandy, as was to be expected, had entered Nirvana. Her eyes, fixed on mine, shone with a fervour of fulfilment and gratitude. Then, still looking at me, she began to moan.

I swallowed and glanced away uncomfortably. The noise was embarrassingly personal, high-pitched, jerky, and laboured. One could only hear in it complete submission; the willingness to be used by her man in any way he saw fit.

'Good girl,' Rod grunted throatily, and redoubled his

efforts.

I'd never watched anyone make love before. I wondered whether there was a law against it; indecency, or something. I was beginning to get very hot inside the mask and I could begin to feel drops of perspiration dribbling down my neck. I could hear the regular thwack as Rod's pelvis thudded savagely against Mandy's sore buttocks. Her whole body jerked forward spasmodically, driving her face ever harder against the bed cover. But still she stared into my eyes, the disgusting noise escaping from her lips in a persistent whine, exaggerated by each subsequent blow.

I became so embarrassed that I tried to think of myself as a detached observer trying to absorb useful hints on technique, rather than as an accomplice in setting up the whole sordid affair. Was Mandy a good lover? I wondered. Hardly. She seemed to be totally passive, her only contribution being the willingness to have her body completely subjugated and overwhelmed.

What about Rod, then? He was a professional and should know his business thoroughly. Was he employing any subtlety I should be aware of, or just his huge, obedient prick?

He was still staring fixedly at me, as if entranced by the novelty of the situation. At one point he grinned and nodded lewdly at my bosom. I glanced down and was appalled to see that my breasts had sprouted telltale turrets, proclaiming my involvement and – as he would assume – my enjoyment of the tableau. Worse, I noticed that because my knees were pressed against the bed in the tiny room my body was shaking rhythmically too, and my breasts were bouncing enticingly.

Then he too started to groan, a strained grunting that was even more shameless than Mandy's eager mewling. At last his eyes dropped from my body and fixed themselves on her beleaguered rump. His jaw clenched with effort and he lengthened his stride. That did not seem to me a possible thing to do until I realised he was now completely withdrawing his member on every stroke, forcing it back in with bullying accuracy and savage force on the next.

'Jesus, Mandy, this is so good,' I heard him cough.

That was all the encouragement she needed to finally discard her last shreds of restraint. Her cries became hoarser and louder, till the tiny room seemed full of nothing else. And worse, I was now a part of it. I found myself moaning in sympathy with Mandy, hurried gasps of pleasure and excitement that had no place in a lady's repertoire. The heat was appalling and perspiration covered my whole body. But the moisture between my legs was not perspiration, I knew. It was slut juice, brought on not by any normal physical stimulation, but simply by the sight of two humans copulating.

The urgency in Rod's gasps suddenly increased alarmingly. With a noise not unlike a wounded sea-lion he threw three or four huge thrusts, before one last determined pile-driver that left him draped over Mandy's back, exhausted and fulfilled.

At last the noise abated and all was silent, except for the hoarse breathing of three heaving chests.

Rod rolled off Mandy and pulled her over onto her back. I now witnessed possibly the most extraordinary part of the entire episode. Rod covered her face with kisses and murmured endearments in her ear, belatedly producing the sexual foreplay that should have preceded the engagement. I realised that I had literally seen two people fall for each other. At some point in the proceedings Rod had stopped acting and become utterly captivated by Mandy. After years of making love under contract he had for the first time experienced the overwhelming involvement that utter commitment brings.

I knew there was no longer any part for me to play, so as quietly as I could I picked up my dressing gown, put it on, and let myself apologetically out of the door.

# Chapter Five

When I got back to my room it dawned on me that I was still wearing Rod's mask. I took it off and turned to put it on the bedside table, when with a shock I saw that there was someone in my bed. It was Astrud, the girl I had sat next to at dinner. She had been asleep, but my return woke her and she sat up sleepily, displaying naked shoulders and breasts.

'Please don't be angry, Lady Sarah,' she said, yawning cutely. 'I couldn't bear being on my own in a strange house. This place scares me, so I crept in here. You'd left the door unlocked.'

Once again I couldn't demand that she leave without appearing ridiculously prudish. Besides, I felt much the same way about Athelstan as she did. I recalled that it had been a frequent practice at Westover for girls to share beds for company or warmth. So I took my dressing gown off, and considered getting my nightie out of a drawer. But that would look far too formal, so in the end I slipped into the bed, also naked.

'Call me Sally,' I said. 'Lady sounds so silly.'

Before I had even settled down her arms were around me and I felt her hands on my body.

'I've got a scrapbook of your wedding at home, you know,' she whispered. 'I couldn't believe how beautiful you are. A princess. And here you are, with me, in this awful hellhole. Why on earth did you get sent here?'

I gave a hollow laugh and said, 'I didn't. I came of my own free will. Can you believe that? I had no idea I was going to be embarrassed and bullied half to death.'

I rolled over to face her and felt the soft, unconstrained melange of our breasts. To my consternation this peculiar sensation brought back a rush of memories I would prefer to have discarded. I snuggled down comfortably against her and waited for sleep, long overdue, to consume me. But the images fidgeted through my brain.

Lindos.

Where the sultry smell of oleander and the warm sunshine and gentle breezes had stripped me of my customary caution. Saved by the bell – or rather, a knock on the door.

When Megan had come back from the restaurant's rather unsavoury loo she found us all missing. Suspicious of Simon and Piers' motives she had cleverly enlisted the help of the tour's local rep, a blond Adonis called Alan. He had apparently been reluctant to intervene, having assumed correctly that Megan had been cruelly dropped by the lads in favour of sweeter fruit. However, she pointed out that I was under eighteen and that he was therefore to some degree responsible for me. So Alan reluctantly checked his guest list till he found two punters named Simon and Piers. Then he and Megan went round to their room armed with the pass key.

What met their eyes when they burst in was not a pretty sight, especially for a conscientious tour rep. A naked girl, completely insensible, lay on the boys' bed while they, though still fully dressed, had obviously been indulging in whatever diversions took their fancy. The smell of marijuana hung heavy in the air and an expensive Japanese camera, equipped with a flash, lay close by, establishing their evil intentions beyond question.

I learned all this the next day. When Megan and Alan interrupted us and it became clear that the drama was over, that spark of consciousness I had clung to finally deserted me and I really did pass out. With hangovers all round the following morning, I heard that the boys were in deep trouble. Criminal charges would be brought, Alan told me, no doubt expecting my gratitude.

In one way he was right. In the cold light of day I was utterly appalled at how close to total violation I had come, though I had not the slightest intention of letting anyone know how long I had remained conscious. But when I heard that the two lads were languishing in a Greek jail I started feeling more than a little guilty at my part in the fiasco. As the boys had said, no one forced me to drink all that wine, or to go back to their room, or to smoke their marijuana. So in their defence I insisted that I was still a virgin.

'Are you sure?' asked Alan.

'Of course,' I replied, vehemently.

I could see that no one was going to believe me. I had, after all, been completely insensible by the time Megan and Alan arrived on their mission of mercy. The issue hung in the balance. The boys *had* been dressed, after all. The only way to resolve it appeared to be for me to undergo a detailed medical examination. I was appalled but overruled. They could not take my word for it and the lads' futures were literally at stake.

I was ushered – perhaps frog-marched would be more accurate – into the consulting room of the local Greek doctor, where I endured one of the worst half-hours of my life. I simply froze – there's no other word for it. Every touch from the doctor's hands seemed to tear me apart. Don't get the wrong idea; there was nothing medically improper about the examination – indeed, there was a nurse present. However, she only made my self-consciousness worse. And the poor doctor could not reassure me with the usual 'this won't take a minute, my dear', because I could not understand him.

My problem was purely psychological, but none the less painful for that. Mentally I could not cope with the idea of somebody examining my private parts, especially after the degradation of the previous night.

So I came out of the consultation pale and trembling, like a ghost. When the doctor confirmed my intactness I swore roundly at Alan. 'What did I tell you? I should know whether I'm a fucking virgin or not!' I shouted.

So the boys escaped jail, though they were packed off home on the next available flight, without compensation.

Alan became strangely solicitous after this episode, searching me out, even on the beach, and asking me at every possible opportunity if everything was in order. At last he made his big play.

'I have to check out a new restaurant for the company,' he informed me almost apologetically, 'to see whether it meets the standard for inclusion on our list of recommended venues. Would you care to come with me?'

I didn't recollect having been given any such list when I arrived, but I didn't say so. As I've hinted, Alan was pretty dishy in a nervous sort of way, and he had a suntan the colour of Brown Windsor soup. Why fight it? I thought. At least it would make all the other girls jealous.

The evening started well enough. The establishment – another of Lindos' many roof garden restaurants – was desperate to please, knowing how important Alan's recommendation could be to them. They treated us like royalty, showing us round the kitchen, insisting we sample all the dishes. And of course I got drunk again. We were so wrapped up in trying the tsatziki and the swordfish that I scarcely noticed how much I was putting away. And this time it wasn't Retsina, but a local wine of a much higher calibre.

When Alan produced the inevitable invitation back to his room for a brandy I was drunk enough to accept, but not drunk enough to give up all resistance. If he'd been a little less nervous and a little more accomplished as a lover I've no doubt he could have breached my defences; it did pass through my mind while I was pushing his hands away for the umpteenth time that I was refusing an offer most girls would have killed for. But he was under a severe constraint himself; he had just packed two paying customers off back home because they had pursued their nefarious aims too hard. And here he was, with the same aims, the same victim, and with a similar degree of aggression. If I'd been a couple of years younger the epithet 'jail-bait' would have fitted me perfectly. He knew this and in the end he desisted.

But unfortunately he was saddled with an erection of monumental proportions and potentially infinite persistence.

'Do it with your hand,' he begged, and was actually weeping tears of supplication as he said it.

I could well have replied, 'Do what?' – I was that innocent. But the hundreds of hours of girlish discussion after lights-out at Westover paid off. One of the girls had once described how she jerked off her date in the back of a car.

I was now eager to try the same trick and I went to work on Alan's painfully swollen appendage with perhaps a little too much eagerness. His face twisted into a tortured grimace, grunts escaped from his lips, and his hands clawed frantically at my bosom. Within a very few seconds we got a result and a stream of milky liquid shot literally halfway across the tiny room. The hot spear I was holding then appeared to pant for a few moments as if racked by convulsions. I was pretty certain I'd done Alan a serious injury, but he just buried his face in my hair and kept mumbling, 'Thank you… thank you…'

I also discovered for the first time that once this point-of-no-return has been passed all the tension goes out of the situation. Alan rapidly lost interest and his persistent groping for my lower regions ceased immediately. I also gathered that I was supposed to go home.

Feeling a strong sense of anti-climax, I set off back through the winding streets to my digs.

'I wondered where you'd got to,' said Megan accusingly, as I came in through the door.

'Still a virgin,' I reported, my jaunty sarcasm masking a strange underlying disappointment.

'I should hope so,' she said. 'You don't want to give it away that easily. Not on a package holiday.'

Did she mean it would have been okay on a Mediterranean cruise?

'What've you been doing?' I asked, conversationally.

'Getting drunk,' she confided, showing me a litre carton of orange juice and a large bottle of Metaxa brandy, still more than half full.

'Seems like I've got some catching up to do,' I replied, holding out my tooth glass.

I hadn't, of course, and proceeded to get thoroughly smashed, inwardly reluctant that I'd passed up the opportunity to get properly rogered. Megan was becoming maudlin.

'You know,' she slurred, 'I was really depressed when you went off with Alan.'

Mere girl talk, I assumed. She just didn't want to be left out of things. I continued to demolish the brandy, unaware that her remark might have a deeper meaning.

'Shit, I can't stand,' I complained, after another couple of glasses of the lethal mixture. 'How am I to make it to bed?'

'I'll help you,' answered Megan eagerly, ignoring the fact that mine had been purely a rhetorical question.

And she did. Fingers fumbled with my clothes, and I had the strange impression that a pair of lips had lightly brushed my buttocks.

'It's too hot for a sheet tonight,' I announced as I fell forward onto the bed, on my face. 'Wake me up at noon.'

Was I pretending? I don't think so. I seemed to have got into the same semi-conscious euphoric haze I had managed with Simon and Piers, limbs helpless but a dim awareness still hovering somewhere behind my eyes.

I felt Megan climb onto the bed next to me. Fair enough. It was her bed too.

I knew her naked body was pressing against mine, but then I'd flopped down selfishly in the middle. She had no room. But what was her hand doing, resting lightly on my bottom?

'Are you awake, Sally?' she tried, in a stage whisper.

Awake, but quite incapable of responding.

The situation was similar but my feelings were quite unlike those with Simon and Piers. Megan was incredibly gentle and cautious, almost religious. Her hands crept over my body, lightly, tracing its contours, revelling in the texture of my skin. Perhaps the Greek doctor had been just as gentle. I don't know. I only know that his hands had felt like sandpaper whereas Megan's fingertips reminded me of thistledown, and where they touched me a minute charge of electricity seemed to flow between us.

'You're so beautiful, Sally,' she whispered in my ear. 'I wish I were like you.'

You are, I thought, puzzled. You're a girl too, so why are you touching me like this?

Her lips traced the same paths as her fingertips, and I would swear she was crying under her breath. Oh come on, I thought. You're not so badly stacked yourself. Then I remembered Piers' remark about perfection in looks. Megan had all the right swellings, but they just didn't hang together the way mine did.

There was no magic there.

Magic? What was I saying? How big headed I was getting! But I had genuinely begun to realise just how awesome my endowments were, and more importantly, how strong was the attraction such looks could exert, not only on men, but evidently on women too. I had often stared at myself in the mirror, and what I saw was a slim, well-proportioned body, but one where, paradoxically, the flesh seemed almost to be trying to burst out of the skin. There was just a tiny hint of chubbiness there, enough to make hands long to reach out and touch but never enough to destroy the impression of perfection.

Megan could see it too. Presently she climbed astride me and began to massage my back. I loved it. Gone was any fear or guilt. I was unconscious, so she supposed, therefore whatever she was doing to me was for her enjoyment, not mine. Presently she lay down full length on my back. It was an odd position, unlikely, I should have thought, to impart any pleasure. But strangely I felt her softness like a huge protective shield cutting me off from the rest of the world. It was sexy as hell.

But it was hot. We kept the window closed to discourage mosquitoes. Now the atmosphere was heavy and erotic. I could feel the sweat building up between our bodies. Megan gave the back of my neck one last kiss, then slid sideways off me, back onto the bed. Her hand once again traced a slow path down my back, but this time it came to rest just between my legs. I waited for her fingers to invade me, but she seemed to have lost her nerve.

I counted another minute go by, but nothing happened. This is no good, I thought. I'm all sexed up. With a heavy sigh, as if I was still asleep, I rolled onto my side, facing her, pressing my belly and chest against hers.

'Oh yes, sweet Sally,' she murmured. 'Touch me.'

Our breasts were crushed together, a strange but not unpleasant squidgy feeling. I felt her take hold of my right hand. I wondered whether she was going to pull it onto her breast, but perhaps she felt, as I did, that naked bosoms in close contact need no embellishment. Instead she dragged it down between her legs.

Now this was tricky. I was supposed to be unconscious. How could I show interest without revealing my deception and thereby destroying the magic? I solved the problem by pretending to be subconsciously aroused. I gave a series of stifled groans and slipped one of my fingers sleepily into her honeypot.

What on earth am I doing? I wondered. This is disgusting. And indeed it was, but strangely exciting too. Soft, slippery flesh lay beneath my fingers, slimy to the touch, but hot and inviting. I fumbled about till I happened upon a swollen button that seemed determined to be fondled. Megan's sudden frightened gasps told me that I had indeed found the spot; that raw, erotic nerve.

Her lips closed over mine and the groans torn from the back of her throat would surely have woken even the most paralytic drunkard, but still I maintained my pretence. As I hoped, Megan's courage returned. Her hand slid between my thighs and her fingers searched out and toyed with my core in just the same way as I was fondling her.

I'm in heaven, I thought.

The previous night had been different. Even though I had been unwillingly aroused into wishing the boys would make love to me, there had remained that fear of the unpredictability of the male. No such danger existed here, and I was able simply to enjoy the experience. Megan's attentions soon had my emotions rising to such a level that I had to stifle the gasps that sprang unbidden to my lips.

Although I was boiling over with lust I still had to show some restraint.

After all, being insensible was what made it fun, and what had given Megan the courage to get this far. Trouble was, I wanted her to go further. I gave one last exaggerated groan and then slid happily and comfortably into what I hoped would appear to be a deep sleep. Megan relaxed too and began to cover my body with kisses, giving my nipples more than their fair share of attention.

Lazily I rolled onto my back, allowing my legs to fall slightly apart, almost as an invitation. As if reading my mind, Megan gave my navel a tickle with her tongue and then worked unhurriedly down. I felt myself trembling in anticipation.

What a difference there was between Megan's languid approach and the boys' eagerness! She paused for an age at the doorway, her lips brushing the luxuriant tawny bush that protected it from the casual glance. Then she pushed that aside, slid down off the end of the bed and onto the floor, and insinuated her head cautiously between my thighs. I pretended to resist, but she was gently insistent and soon I could feel her lips and tongue dancing lightly over my sensitive entrance.

I realised that she was well practised in this art of stimulation, despite her tender age, and that I was not the first to have benefited from her agile tongue and her obsession with the female body. She not only found my pleasure button and disturbed its peace of mind, she also played tricks on me that extracted pleasures more diffuse but no less delightful. I felt as though I were floating a foot above the bed, powered by emotion alone.

I could no longer suppress the urgent gasps that leaped from my throat, but I supposed that such a reaction would be the natural one for a young woman so expertly aroused, even if stupefied by drink. So I allowed my groans to grow in volume along with Megan's excitement, and I even reached sleepily down till my hands were holding her head, coaxing her to greater extremes. My breath sawed deeply in and out of my lungs and my head began to roll from side to side.

One huge satisfied sigh signalled my culmination, and judging from the eager attentions of Megan's lips I had established that at least some girls relish pineapple juice as much as boys. My hands pulled her head urgently against me.

My muscles were evidently obeying my brain.

Oh dear, the truth had come out! I was not really unconscious at all, I at last admitted to myself. I was simply a shameless slut!

# Chapter Six

Monday morning at Athelstan Hall. I awoke to find my arms still clasping Astrud's soft body. I shook her gently.

'Wake up,' I whispered. 'We're late for breakfast. We'll probably get spanked, or something.'

I found her some of my clothes to wear and we hurried downstairs to discover that we were indeed the last to the feast – and that it was extremely meagre.

Corn flakes, toast and marmalade, a cup of instant coffee, and that was it.

And there was no sign of Mandy. I had not forgotten that she was to take me into town this morning.

Sister Murdock appeared from the kitchen and clapped her hands for attention. 'Ladies,' she called. 'I'm afraid I have a very serious announcement.'

There was a rustle of apprehension. From the tone of her voice someone was in for a heavy scolding.

'I awoke this morning to find that Mandy, our cook and waitress, and Rod, our normally obedient eagle, have disappeared. I went up to Mandy's room but found it empty. There was also evidence of an erotic tryst. I think we have to assume that they have run off together.

'Needless to say, I am extremely angry about this, not least because I myself have had to prepare the rather substandard breakfast you received this morning. Staff should give notice. That's part of their contract. However, as with so many things these days, no one takes any notice of etiquette, or even terms of employment.'

I was furious, too. Mandy had promised to help me. But evidently she had become so enamoured with her new conquest that she had decamped without even so much as a goodbye or a thank you.

But Sister Murdock had more to say.

'In Mandy's room I found this.'

She held up the silken rope that acted as the cord for my dressing gown.

'I want to know to whom this belongs. It is clearly not Mandy's, it's far too expensive. I am not going to pursue any investigation as to what unsavoury purpose it was put to last night. However, I do require to know who's it is.'

I swallowed nervously. This was just like being back at school; own up, or I'll keep the whole class in after games.

Trouble was, I had a pretty shrewd notion she had already guessed it was mine. I did not want to be made to look foolish by her gleefully revealing my guilt and calling me a liar and a coward.

So I stood up.

'It's mine, Sister Murdock,' I admitted.

'Thank you, Lady Sarah,' she said, with no surprise in her expression. 'I'm very glad you owned up. I had already found Rod's bald eagle mask in your room, so I had little doubt as to who was the culprit. You have apparently incited Rod and Mandy to leave. I don't know why, but I am, as I said, very angry. Your forfeit, which is entirely appropriate, is to take Mandy's place in the kitchen this morning, and as waitress at lunchtime. I hope you haven't already become such a grand lady that you can no longer wash up breakfast dishes, or cook lunch. And for your sake, I hope that by that time I will have been able to get a replacement from the town.'

Trapped again. I knew she had absolutely no right to demand that one of her paying guests act the part of a servant. But if I refused I would be branded as a spoiled brat. Determined not to give her that pleasure I simply shrugged and began to gather up the cereal bowls.

'I'll help you,' whispered Astrud.

So she and I cleared the big refectory table while Sister Murdock ushered the rest of the girls away in the direction of the gym. It occurred to me that Astrud and I might be in for a less arduous time, doing kitchen chores, than trying to meet Sister Murdock's unreasonable demands on the exercise machines.

'Mandy promised to help me escape,' I told Astrud, angrily. 'She said she had to take the car into town this morning and that she would smuggle me out in it. So much for promises.'

As I said it I remembered something that Mandy had said *after* she'd made the offer the previous night. 'You'll see plenty more beatings before your week's out'. That should have warned me she had already forgotten her promise to help me. How callous!

'I'm glad you didn't get away,' Astrud said shyly as she accepted the washed dishes from me, one by one, and dried them.

'What do you mean?' I asked.

'I – um – I think I'm in love with you,' she blabbered.

'What? That's absurd!' I burst. 'I'm a married woman, with the best husband anyone could hope for!'

'That doesn't matter,' she persisted. 'I don't expect you to love me.'

I was at a loss for words. Then I had a sudden insight.

'Astrud, why are you in here?' I asked. 'You said it was your husband's doing. Was it a punishment for going with another woman?'

It was obvious from her face that I was right. She eventually nodded miserably.

'Jerry came home early one evening and found me dancing in the nude with Marcie, one of the neighbours I met at a coffee morning,' she confessed. 'He said he was sending me here to teach me a lesson.'

'Even so, he's got no right to punish you physically,' I said. 'It's against the law, surely, to force your spouse to go somewhere against their will.'

'You're probably right,' she agreed lamely. 'But he said he'd leave me if I didn't obey. Jerry says he'll send me back in here any time he finds me cheating on him.'

'Then you shouldn't be making improper suggestions to me,' I pointed out.

'Why not? I'm already in here. Things can't get any worse.'

'They might,' I said grimly. 'Sister Murdock might start picking on you instead of me.'

Astrud laughed. 'You're right,' she said. 'She's really got her teeth into you, *Lady* Sarah.'

It came home to me that after my failure to escape with Mandy's help this was now really no laughing matter, and I was suddenly swept by that awful dread a victim of bullying gets when there's no chance of running away.

'Is it going to get worse, do you think?' I asked. 'She can't surely be serious about beating us.'

Astrud paused for a long time, holding a dripping coffee cup, then nodded sympathetically. 'I think you have to expect the worst. One of the girls – Elspeth, the redhead –

said that whoever pays for you to come here can specify how much punishment you should receive, and that he can demand some sort of proof – photographs, or whatever – that it has indeed been carried out.'

'But that's appalling!' I exclaimed.

'I know,' she agreed, nodding. 'I hope it's not true.'

I looked round desperately at the kitchen windows, but they were all barred. 'Have you tried to get out?' I asked.

She shook her head 'What would be the use? SM would tell Jerry and I'd be back in here at the start of next week. And with a big black cross against my name marking me out for special treatment.'

Maybe not, I thought. Her husband didn't own her. If we could get out we could go to the police and have the place closed down for good.

Astrud put away the last of the breakfast dishes and mopped her brow symbolically. 'Whew, that's done,' she said. 'Why don't we nip upstairs for a nice shower before we get on with preparing the lunch?'

It was a sensible suggestion, since we'd both dashed down for breakfast without even washing. But after that strange avowal of love I suspected she might have something a bit sideways in mind.

'I suspect you of some ulterior motive,' I said candidly, voicing my concerns.

'Is that a "no", then?' she said.

''Fraid so,' I told her. 'You go and have a wash. I'll get started on the lunch.'

'Are you scared of me?' she suddenly asked.

'Of course not,' I said.

'So what's the problem?'

'You know…' I ventured awkwardly, 'you said you were

in love with me.'

'I am,' she insisted. 'That's why I want to have a shower with you. But nothing dreadful is going to happen, is it?'

'I – I don't know,' I said, feeling confused.

'The worst I could do is touch you,' she said, almost mocking me. 'Come on, loosen up.'

I shook my head.

Astrud thought for a moment. 'Do you really want to get out of Athelstan?' she asked.

'Yes,' I confirmed with determination.

'Then I might be able to help you.'

'Tell me.'

'No,' she teased. 'We have to have the shower first. Then I'll tell you.'

Even though it didn't sound very convincing, I was intrigued and immediately capitulated.

We went back up to my room, picked up some towels and soap, and went into the deserted bathroom area. There were six showers in a tiled area, three on each side. I undressed nervously, aware that Astrud was staring at me. I slipped under the hot water and then watched as she stripped off. A female body is always a fascinating sight. How would she compare with me?

She was not as tall as me, and was a little plumper, though not unpleasantly so. She was very pink and warm looking, compared to my deep bronze tan. When she was naked she walked straight under my shower.

'Give me a kiss,' she demanded.

'Hey!' I objected, 'we're just here for a wash, right?'

'Relax,' she soothed, 'I can't hurt you, can I?'

She put her arms round me and hugged our bodies together so that the water formed a temporary pond between our breasts, arms, and shoulders. I reluctantly gave her the kiss she wanted. I was not in any way afraid of her, of course, nor did the idea of a friendly cuddle disgust me. Far from it. My problem was that I felt that once we started we might not stop. Ever since my behaviour in Lindos I had been seriously worried that I might be a latent lesbian. I did not want such feelings to get in the way of my relationship with Peter, and the best way to avoid that seemed to be to avoid temptation in the first place.

But Astrud clearly had no such inhibitions. She found a bar of soap and began washing my back, her body still pressed against mine. Shoulders and spine received her concentrated attention, followed by waist and bottom. Then, when her hands delved between my buttocks she became even slower and more thorough.

'Astrud…' I murmured, embarrassed.

Her response was simply to push a finger even harder against my tight, apprehensive flower. 'Yield,' she commanded. 'Come on, stop being so stuffy.'

Miserable at my own self-consciousness, I simply shut my eyes and let my muscles go limp. Her finger slipped inside and she probed around.

'There you are,' she breathed, 'that wasn't so bad, was it? Clean, inside and out.'

The water continued to pour over us and the steam mercifully hid my blushing face from her stare. Now she started on my front, using a large soapy flannel to push and tease my breasts, exaggerating their fluidity. My stomach was next, with my navel enjoying a fresh clean lease of life. Down she went, working the soap into my reddish-golden bush, scrubbing till the skin beneath tingled. As the relentless cascade washed me clean, so she dropped to her knees, brushing my curls with her lips. Her fingers invaded me from the front and once again she probed. I gasped at the sheer intimacy of the action and my knees began to tremble from nervous anticipation. My intent to avoid erotic contact had been as feeble as my protestations when she originally proposed a shower.

She continued on down, washing my thighs, knees and calves. She pushed her body between my legs and sat on the tiled floor, washing my feet. Then she lay on her back staring up at me, almost exactly between my legs.

'Can you go for me?' she asked.

She could only mean one thing! Poor Lady Sarah was stunned and horrified by the suggestion. But Sally the slut had already woken from her sleep, aroused by Astrud's intimate caresses, and she was immediately intrigued by the idea.

What Astrud was asking for should have been unthinkable, and would have been in any normal surroundings.

But nothing was normal in Athelstan Hall.

Sarah reflected on the practicalities of the request. I'd had plenty of coffee for breakfast, and an orange juice. There was no problem doing what Astrud wanted. Sally found such calculations unnecessary – she knew what I could or could not do.

The pale golden flood spilled out, mixing with the shower water and pouring down over Astrud's face and body. Her eyes closed in ecstasy and her tongue reached up, sampling the precious fluid. I kept going as long as I could, but eventually the stream ran out and I stood there, knees shaking, heart pumping, trembling from some strange nervous exhaustion.

Astrud got to her feet and rinsed herself off. I knew why I was nervous. The strange ritual was her equivalent of making us blood sisters. It made no sense unless we both did the same.

And I was right.

'Now it's your turn,' she said quietly.

'Astrud…' I said, mortified, 'I just can't.'

'It'll be over in a moment,' she persisted.

But I'm a nice girl, I wanted to reply. The trouble was, the more inappropriate and disgusting the action I was expected to perform, the more it fascinated me. For Sally, the idea of submitting to Astrud was hypnotic.

If I do this thing, she argued, just this one quick act, then no one can ever call me a prude again. Of course, nobody other than myself had called me a prude in the first place. But such logic was of no interest to Sally. She was overwhelmed by the thrill of self-debasement.

So I took a deep breath and lay on my back on the hard tiled floor, the cleansing spray from the shower stinging my face with its force. To my surprise Astrud did not adopt the same position I had held, but instead faced the other way so that she was looking towards my feet. Then she lowered herself unhurriedly. The invitation was clear. I reached up, grasped her hips, and pulled her down onto me, straining my face up eagerly. The water poured down her back and into my eyes. I groped through the turmoil with my tongue and encountered a bitter taste through the confusing flood. I felt her body stiffen with excitement.

She paused, supported in space on her bent knees, then descended onto me with her full weight.

I felt sublimely happy. I could not really understand why,

but I supposed it was the relief from the strain of acting the part of Lady Sarah over the last couple of weeks. This brutal submission was my punishment for being so lucky.

But it was also a reward.

Her generous buttocks, that were now smothering my face, were for a short time shutting out the pain and effort of being civilised in an intensely critical world. For five minutes I could be pure slut. At that thought my own juice immediately began to flow and I felt it being washed away by the shower, going to waste.

Perhaps Astrud sensed this. She slowly leaned forward until at last I could see the light and breathing once again became a possibility. Her hands gently prised my thighs apart and her head pushed its way between them. I tensed nervously, but when her gentle tongue caressed me I gave a sigh of pleasure and let myself relax. We lay in that position for a long time, teasing each other, tickling and probing. I was able to examine another woman's most intimate centre, enjoying both its complexity and simplicity, my tongue flitting from one orifice to the other in response to the shudders of pleasure I felt in her body.

At last, when we were both sated, she lifted herself a few inches off me, straddling me on all fours.

'Are you ready?' she asked.

'Yes, Astrud,' I replied, staring eagerly up at her.

The jet struck me with what seemed like an extraordinary force, so that I gasped with shock, even though I had been expecting it. For a moment I coughed and spluttered but then I regained control of myself and was able to drink down much of the nectar that poured over me. Vague but pleasurable memories of first form games at Westover came back to me. How exciting it had been, I remembered, to accept a 'dare' to perform an act the other girls found too disgusting! Now my heady submersion lacked only that circle of awed faces to make the reconstruction perfect. But my enjoyment couldn't last forever. Eventually the flow dried up and I was left desperately licking at its source, trying to catch the last drops before the shower washed them away.

Good, I thought happily. Very good. There was no way I could ever sink lower than that.

# Chapter Seven

When we had tidied ourselves up and dressed, I asked her the burning question that was still uppermost in my mind.

'What is this idea of yours for escaping?'

She snorted. 'Oh, I don't know whether it's any good.'

'Don't you let me down too,' I complained. 'You *do* have an idea, don't you?'

'Yes, yes,' she insisted. 'What I mean is that I can't guarantee it'll work. Thing is, there's a gardener. He spends most of his time alone in the grounds, working on the lawns or the flowerbeds. But yesterday I happened to see him indoors, eating his sandwiches. Presumably the old witch is too mean to let him have what the guests eat.'

'You mean, he must have a key!' I squealed excitedly.

'Well, I imagine so,' she said. 'I arrived before the rest of the guests, and I was passing the time exploring the house. I stumbled into this tiny utility room at the very far end. It has a door directly to the outside. He was in there. You've got plenty of money. Seems to me all you've got to do is nip along there this afternoon and establish just how big a bribe he needs to let you out.'

I was so pleased I sent her off to join the others while I prepared lunch by myself. And with such high spirits the work flew by. I had to make twelve individual pizzas for the guests and the favoured staff, namely Sister M and the three remaining studs.

The peculiar thing was how much I enjoyed doing it,

simply because it was hard work. I started out thinking that I would have to force myself to get the job done, just to prove to Sister Murdock that I wasn't a helpless spoiled bitch. But there's nothing so good for the soul as creating something by your own efforts – even if it's going to be eaten within the next hour. I recognised that my new role as Lady Sarah was glaringly devoid of any such achievements, and that even after a couple of weeks I had begun to get bored, though I'd been careful not to admit it.

I knew I would also have to be the waitress. That meant I could give any particular pizza to whomever I chose. The temptation for some silliness was too great. I marked the edge of one pizza base with a nick that would identify it as Sister Murdock's. I was still hot and wet from the session with Astrud. So, looking round apprehensively, I flipped up my skirt, dropped my briefs and sat squarely on Sister Murdock's pizza base, impregnating it, I hoped, with a unique flavour which unfortunately I had to admit would be unlikely to survive the baking.

I spent the rest of the morning giggling at the stupidity of what I'd done. By twelve-thirty I had a dozen golden-brown pizzas, hot from the oven, complemented by some tuna salad which I put out on the table in advance as a starter, together with several carafes of a delectable Italian red wine, which I had not failed to taste two or three times to make sure it would chambré correctly. By now I was so pleased with myself and so certain I would be off the premises in an hour that I could not bear simply to serve the food meekly as Mandy had. I must think of something outrageous.

The philosophy of Athelstan Hall was that of punishment

and subjugation, I reflected, with Sister Murdock as its perverted provider. In my slightly tipsy haze it seemed to me that I would score handsomely over her if I pre-empted her bullying and instead subjugated myself willingly.

I nipped upstairs for the eagle mask that was still in my room, and also a pair of shoes with absurdly high heels. In the privacy of the kitchen I slipped out of my clothes and put on only the large red plastic apron I had used for cooking. From the front I was perfectly decent, but from the rear I was stark naked. With the mask and the shoes I was ready for my customers, if only I could stop giggling. I had, I reflected, been in the madhouse for less than twenty-four hours, yet I seemed already to have lost my grip on reality.

I carried the first two pizzas in, to a round of light applause. But when I turned to go back to the kitchen Astrud, who was still watching me, gave an enormous shriek of disbelief, and soon all the girls were convulsed with laughter too.

After they had all been served I was left with four plates for Sister Murdock and the three lads. They ate in their own little staff-room just down the corridor. I tapped on the door and heard Sister Murdock tell the others to put their masks on. It was evidently one of the house rules that the guests must never see a stud's face.

'Come in,' she called.

I pushed the door open and carried in the first two dishes. As before my arrival excited no more reaction than amusement that I was wearing the eagle's head. But when I turned to walk back to the kitchen I heard a most gratifying series of gasps as my back came into view.

I returned with the second pair of pizzas, one of which

was for Sister Murdock. This time I knew things wouldn't be quite so easy. I walked into the room, head bowed demurely. Then I almost exclaimed out loud with annoyance.

While I was out of the room Lance, the dragon, had politely passed his pizza over to Sister Murdock. Ladies first. How silly of me not to have thought of that! Well, there was nothing I could do about it now. I could not swap plates without making my trick obvious, so I put the doctored pizza down in front of Spike.

'Enjoy your lunch,' I said to him.

Then I turned to go, but Sister Murdock called me back. 'Sarah, come over here, my dear.'

Reluctantly I walked over and stood beside her. Immediately I felt a hand sliding up my thigh. Then there was another, fondling my legs and buttocks. I stood straight and proud. I would not give them the pleasure of making me flinch away.

'I want to congratulate you, Sarah, on an excellent lunch,' she said. 'You have not only reacted commendably in the face of my petty forfeit, you have risen above it. Your outfit is a credit to Athelstan Hall and to yourself. You are a very plucky young lady.'

There was a pause. The hands continued their exploration and were getting perilously close to places only Peter and I had a right to touch.

'Very well,' she concluded. 'You may go.'

I walked stiffly from the room, determined not to hurry. I felt justifiably proud of my self-control. I had come a long way since that Greek doctor examined me in Lindos.

After lunch was eaten I cleared away and found myself with time to think. I was able to do the washing-up while keeping an eye on the window. I could see the gardener in the distance, much too far away to get an impression of his face, but I would easily be able to spot him when he came in for his snack.

Meanwhile, I decided to continue with my interrupted self-analysis. I had really behaved very recklessly. Could it be that I was actually overcoming the shyness I blamed for my persistent virginity?

I thought back and realised that my behaviour had always been very much influenced by my environment. Whilst serving lunch, with those male hands mauling me, I had been wearing the eagle mask and that had made an enormous difference to my confidence. When Simon and Piers had me in their power I had been 'hidden' behind the mask of intoxication. I poured myself another large glass of wine, and relaxed by its Italian warmth, I now had the courage to recall another disgraceful episode where I was merely hidden behind dark sunglasses, but where their presence had undoubtedly contributed to my uninhibited attitude.

When Megan and I awoke the morning after our licentious fondling the atmosphere was distinctly edgy. Megan stared at me with adoration and I could tell she was hoping for an avowal of love, though she was too scared to offer one herself. But with the return of sanity had come also my self-consciousness. I could not bring myself to admit what had happened, even though I had enjoyed it. Instead I played dumb.

'Jesus, we certainly had a skinful last night,' I said with

a wry grin. 'I was out cold. Had a hell of a sexy dream, though.'

Hope showed in Megan's eyes, but disappointment too. Naked, I got out of bed and went into the bathroom to clean my teeth. I had some serious thinking to do. I was worried about my extreme adverse reaction to the Greek doctor's hands on my body when contrasted to the previous night's skin-tingling cornucopia of lust. It seemed there was some good news and some bad news. Some simple gymnastics with fingers and tongue had transported me effortlessly to Nirvana.

No reason not to make the journey again, whenever I wanted.

The fact that my body seemed to function as nature intended, perhaps even a little more warmly than was strictly necessary, should hardly have been a cause for distress. But it had taken me a long time to put two and two together. I had discovered sex. The seriously bad news was that I appeared to be a lesbian. I felt a deep sense of disappointment but the evidence was unarguable. I had, in retrospect, been terrified by my exposure to Simon and Piers. I'd done little else in the succeeding days except think about how it might have felt if they'd had their way with me.

In contrast, I had been easily transported to heaven the previous night by a nondescript girl I had known for years. The reason was obvious. Megan was safe. I had not been overcome by that terrifying tremble that had dogged my earlier outings with boys. I had instead been able to lie back and enjoy things. The rest of my life was clearly signposted, therefore. I would become part of Chislehurst's thriving gay population, my beauty earning me adulation from any woman to whom I cared to offer it. Until I became too old to pull any more.

What a pity, my other self said. What a shame men are such beasts. Why do they always look at you as though they're about to hit you? Why are their arms quite so strong and muscular? Why do they always have that scary glint in their eye that says they want to fuck you? Still, that's the way life is.

If you don't like it, you keep out of their way. Trouble was, I did like it. In a way. Being scared was exciting. I could never be frightened of Megan. She was too considerate, too obedient. Did I want to flirt with violence, then? Did I want to get hurt? No, of course not. What, then? What was the reason for this residual longing to dabble in men, when common sense said women were so much more enjoyable? It was like following motor racing on the television, I decided. You watched in case there was a crash. When a crash actually happened you didn't necessarily want the driver to get hurt. But unless you believed he might the race had no excitement, no point.

And so with life, evidently. At the age of seventeen I wasn't yet ready to pull over to the slow lane and watch everyone else go by. I would have at least one try with a man, I decided. If that was hopeless, then I would give up for good.

It was well into the morning by the time Megan and I set off for the beach along one of the few routes I could find through the village by myself. The lane was cobbled and deeply ingrained with donkey droppings, and it started off level in a wide circular sweep, following the contour of the steep hillside on which the town was built. Brilliant whitewashed walls lined the road initially, but then suddenly it came out into the open, and to enjoy the view we stopped for a coffee at a little bar overlooking the bay far below. Speedboats were already carving frothy white furrows in the blue sea, and one was pulling a parachute after it, its dangling matchstick figure at about the same height as we were.

'We're late this morning,' I commented, pointing downwards. 'The beach will be full.'

'Damned sunbeds,' grunted Megan. 'Look at them. It's not a beach any more, it's a bloody regimented dormitory.'

I could see what she meant. The sea and the hills in the distance were beautiful. But the sand resembled nothing so much as a car park, with its evenly spaced lines of frying humans filling almost every corner.

'I said we should have gone to Turkey,' I replied, grinning.

'I expect that's just the same,' she grumbled. 'Next year we'll go to Weston-Super-Mare.'

'No way,' I giggled. 'I've already had more fun here than the whole of my previous seventeen years.'

Megan looked extremely miffed. 'You don't call that fiasco with Simon and Piers fun, do you?'

'Well, excitement, then,' I said. 'Come on, let's get down there.'

We paid the meagre bill and I was about to set off down the rock steps to the beach when Megan called me back.

'Look at that,' she said, pointing at the window of a nearby shop, one of those expensive boutiques that contrast strangely with the ramshackle groceries and cafés.

It was a bikini. Well no, just a thong, actually. It had a bottom half only, and even that was virtually non-existent.

It was made of soft woven string, white, but with an absurdly skimpy front triangle of pale blue cotton, not even as large as a lady's handkerchief.

'Nice,' I admitted, impressed.

'You could wear it,' she suggested.

'Don't be silly,' I said, shaking my head.

'Go on,' she persisted. 'I'll buy it for you.'

I stared at her in surprise. Men offered to buy their girlfriends sexy clothes. Other girls did not. The implication was obvious. Megan wanted to show me off. She wanted to lie next to me on the beach with all the men ogling us. She wanted to say, 'This is mine. This is the girl I share a bed with every night.'

Was I angry? No, of course not. I was highly flattered. In fact, I had that now familiar bubbling in my stomach at the idea of flaunting myself to that degree. I imagined my mother glaring at me disapprovingly, perhaps even bursting into tears in sheer dismay. So what? She wasn't there. No one I knew was there, except Megan, and she'd already shown herself prepared to sink to depths of depravity that made a beach thong look like a mere dirty mac.

What a thrill it would be! I longed to wear it, desperately and irrationally.

I wanted grown men to drool at me like spotty teenagers. I wanted to feel their eyes on me while Megan covered my naked buttocks with suntan lotion. I wanted them to go back to their rooms at the end of the day and bang their wives sadly and brutally, thinking all the time of my curved buttocks and what lay between them.

'All right,' I said abruptly. 'But we'll buy it between us. We can wear it on alternate days.'

That was strangely sexy, too; the idea of that slender thong lying first against my private bits, and then Megan's, our scent indiscriminately impregnating the soft white string.

'You first, though,' said Megan, giggling.

'Coward!'

I put it on in the shop's changing cubicle and stared, appalled at the transformation it caused. I could not possibly be seen in something so flagrantly titillating. Then I realised, with horror, that that was precisely why I simply *had* to wear it. It was utterly unwearable. Only a battle-hardened slut could imagine going out in public in that. Therefore I had to prove to myself I could do it. I almost wept with dismay. I had backed myself into a corner. I looked at the mirror again. The eyes that peered back at me were those of a terrified schoolgirl, appalled at what she was contemplating, petrified with fear, though she was as yet alone in the comparative privacy of the changing alcove with only a female friend. I stood there for what seemed like forever.

'I don't have the nerve,' I muttered hopelessly.

'Yes you do,' begged Megan earnestly. 'I'll wear it tomorrow if you'll wear it today.'

An idea. I put my head round the curtain. The shop manager was staring patiently out of the window, the picture of discretion.

'Have you any sunglasses?' I asked.

He handed me a box. I found a pair that wrapped round the sides, covering my eyes completely. I already felt a lot better. I peered out again.

'A sun hat?'

He obliged. My face was now almost entirely obscured.

Perhaps I really could do it, after all. I put my T-shirt and shorts on over the offending costume. My bridges were burned.

We set off down the goat path to the beach, and as we scrambled over the last few rocks we were confronted by one of life's little dramas. An Englishman in baggy Union Jack shorts, with a wife and two small children, had attempted to occupy space on the sand near two wooden fishing boats. The Greek lad who ran the concession for the sunbeds told them they would have to pay the seven hundred drachs, whether or not they used a bed. The man was justifiably angry, but faced with Greek determination he had to back down and eventually he led his family away to the far end of the beach.

'That leaves the space free for us,' I commented mischievously.

I spread my towel on the sand and watched out of the corner of my eye as the Greek lad returned to do battle.

'Seven hundred drachmae,' he said. 'I bring you a sunbed.'

'No thank you,' I replied sweetly. 'We prefer to lie on the sand.'

I discarded my T-shirt and saw his resolution waver. Then off came the shorts and I knew I'd won. His mouth hung open most gratifyingly and he licked his lips nervously. But he couldn't just turn away.

'Would you like a drink?' he asked abruptly.

'Are you buying?' I teased.

'Yes,' he blurted.

'Thank you. I'll have a Gini, please, with plenty of ice, and my friend would like a diet coke.'

He trotted dutifully off to one of the many bars at the

top of the beach to do my bidding. Score one for the thong.

'You stripped off,' murmured Megan, clearly impressed. 'I didn't think you'd have the courage. Shit, now I've got to do it tomorrow.'

So absorbed had I been in my private battle with the Greek boy that I had taken the plunge without even realising it. Now it seemed as if everyone on the beach was staring at me, male and female alike, young and old. I was the star of the show. My terror instantly returned, but having got this far there was no way I could chicken out. I lay down on my stomach and twitched my buttocks brazenly, aware that in comparison with my reluctance to strip-off earlier in the week, I was now remarkably free and easy. Must be the sunglasses.

I had already got thoroughly absorbed in my book when a voice broke in.

'Sorry I am so long. There was a queue.'

It was the Greek lad with our drinks. I was suddenly overcome by guilt. He must have been ten or fifteen minutes at least. And for all I knew the drink from the beachfront café might have cost him half a day's wages. And all because I'd wanted to show off my power.

'Here,' I mumbled, reaching into my bag. 'The seven hundred drachs. Even though I don't want a sunbed.'

'No problem,' he said, waving it away. Then he stood there, tongue-tied, staring at me.

Realisation slowly dawned. This boy fancied me. After all, why else would he buy us drinks? How old was he? Well, younger than me for sure, perhaps not more than sixteen. I was pleasantly amused by the notion that a lad scarcely out of school could be interested in me, already a sophisticated seventeen-year-old.

Then I took a second look at him from behind my glasses. I was being absurd. But still my gaze insisted on wandering over his body.

Well, why not? He was dishy as hell. Look at those black eyes, and that curly hair almost like a girl's, I told myself. And that stomach! Hard, brown, not an ounce of fat. I flushed desperately. A sex fantasy had sprung into my head.

I visualised him from above as he lay face down, naked, his muscular buttocks writhing urgently. With my lack of experience I couldn't be absolutely certain of what he was doing, but I knew that it was me lying under him, my head showing over his shoulder, eyes closed in ecstasy.

I swallowed nervously. No, this was mad. I couldn't really imagine that he would… bonk me. I couldn't bring myself to say the f-word, even in my thoughts. And yet, there he was, waiting. And men will always do it, I'd been told, unless you stop them.

'Phew! Sun's hot,' I said, desperate to break the silence.

'There is a shower,' he said eagerly.

'Really? Where?'

'Up at the hut – the beach-bed store.'

Of course there was absolutely no reason why I shouldn't cool off in the sea. He knew that. I knew that.

'I could kill for a really cold shower,' I lied.

'Come, then.' He set off over the sand without looking behind him.

'I'll be back in a minute,' I said to Megan.

I stumbled to my feet and set off after him, aware of the stares engulfing me. I could hardly walk straight, I felt so giddy. And here I was, following a youth up the beach with mischief on my mind.

I followed him through the doorway of a wooden hut and became immediately blind in the comparative darkness inside. Of course I still had my protective glasses on, so I didn't realise he'd stopped till I walked straight into him. There was a sort of squidgy noise as my bare chest met his, though the softness was all down to me. His body was as hard as a Brazil nut, and even smoother.

'Where's the shower?' I muttered in confusion.

Perhaps it existed, though in retrospect I doubt it. His hands and lips were all over me. All pretence of formality had gone. I gave an involuntary shudder of apprehension as I realised that we really were going to do it. The f-word. I was going to have my insides investigated by this innocent Greek youth.

'What's your name?' I asked breathlessly.

'Tassos,' he grunted angrily, as if wondering why the hell it mattered.

He plainly wasn't going to have the politeness to ask me mine. He pulled me over to the corner of the hut where there was an old wooden table. I realised I was supposed to lie on it. This was definitely not a four-star defloration, but I already seemed to have committed myself so I obliged him. His hands scrabbled at the sides of the thong and pretty soon it was lying, like a discarded snakeskin, on the sand that did service as the floor.

What would it feel like when it went in? I wondered. Was this youth old enough to be fully developed? I would have no idea. But the expected sword failed to skewer me. Instead, to my surprise, my suitor dropped to his knees at the end of the table and his head burrowed its way between my thighs. I realised that his lips were going to do exactly what Piers and Simon had found so exciting.

For a moment I suffered the same stiffening that had caused me such grief in the doctor's. A complete stranger was touching my private parts. A swell of revulsion rose in my throat. But then it occurred to me that maybe the feeling was not entirely unpleasant. Disturbing, perhaps, but not unbearable.

Having nothing better to do with my eyes I peered down to try and appreciate the strange drama of which I was such an integral part. But all I could see was an engrossed mop of black curls framed between two fleshy mountains; assets I had been sure would inspire the devotion of any lover but which were being sadly neglected. My eyes, though still shielded by the sunglasses, were growing accustomed to the gloom. There was a grubby curtain hanging from the ceiling right by the table.

I was wondering vaguely what its purpose was when with a jolt of dismay I notice a pair of feet peeping out from under it. For a second I entertained the hallucination that they were those of my ardent stallion. But that would have required him to be a contortionist and there were, as I now realised, a second pair of feet next to the first...

There could be no doubt. We had company. Okay, so I should be appalled. If I was my mother's daughter I should give a scream of indignation and make a run for the door. Why then, did I feel this strange buzz, this familiar bubbling in my stomach? Surely I couldn't be enjoying lying on my back on a table with a stranger's head between my thighs and half the local population of Lindos looking on? But evidently I was. My baser senses, made hot and horny by the energetic attention of lips and tongue, elbowed sanity out of the window.

Instead I found my hands lasciviously running over my

own body and giving my breasts the stimulation they'd been missing, and just incidentally, giving the onlookers an inkling of just how rich and springy they were. Worse, a choked sigh escaped the back of my throat and pretty soon a continuous groaning filled the tiny hut. It was a disgustingly uninhibited noise. Not me, surely? But if not, then who else?

Surprisingly some dim thread of logic continued to function through all this abandon. Unprompted, that thread recalled the earlier improbable fifteen minutes it had taken Tassos to get my drink. Suddenly its significance struck home. He had obviously run back up to the town to alert his friends to the treat that was to come. And this merely on the strength of my acceptance of one drink! How many sordid little assignations had this rickety table supported? No wonder Tassos had kept his hands to himself! He wanted the audience to have the best possible view of my superstructure. And to think, I'd been apprehensive about depriving him of seven hundred drachs. He was probably charging a thousand a peek!

With an angry snort I sat up, leaned over and wrenched the curtain aside, ready to blister the voyeurs. But I revealed not half the population of Lindos – just two more teenagers looking decidedly shamefaced. Suddenly I burst into laughter. I had behaved like a tart on the beach. Why should I now be so indignant at being treated like one? Besides, these two new lads were every bit as dishy as Tassos.

Scarcely believing what I was doing, I simply lay back again and beckoned. The lads' faces showed first disbelief, then eager lust. They fell upon me greedily, one to each breast, kissing and fondling as if there were no tomorrow.

I gave a happy sigh and abandoned myself to the realm of the senses.

If nature had taken its course I would have lost my virginity at that point. Indeed, I was so overexcited I probably wouldn't even have registered the momentous event occurring. I exhibited not one ounce of the reserve and nervousness I was now showing in response to Peter's advances.

But nature did not take its normal course, and that was entirely my fault. What went wrong was that fairly early on in the proceedings a young and painfully rampant prick passed close before my eyes, and I felt so guilty for having aroused its swollen agony that I gave it a sympathetic kiss. It was both ugly and revolting, I felt, yet it exerted a strange fascination for me, the fascination of the obscene. So the kiss quickly graduated into a playful suck, and before I really knew what was happening I found myself receiving a climactic burst of happiness from the young lad who owned it, and who was staring down into my eyes with grateful disbelief.

Big mistake. Give a man, or even a Greek youth, the choice between a suck and having to work to provide the real thing, and he'll invariably choose the former. The other two boys queued up eagerly after the first to have their own agony kissed better.

I thought nothing of it in the heat of the moment. After all, I still had my dark glasses on, convincing me that some anonymous slut, not me, was performing the actions. And anyway, there was always a third boy free to keep my own pot gratefully boiling. But I had not appreciated how soon male lust is exhausted. Although I would have been quite willing to continue our frantic coupling right through the morning and up to lunchtime, my suitors lacked the stamina. Once they'd shot their loads sanity reasserted itself and with a mumbled thank you – at least I hope that was what they said – they disappeared back to whatever jobs it was they were neglecting.

Eventually I got my breath back and sat up. I was submerged in a sea of discomfort. My nipples hurt from being squeezed by fingers, lips, and even teeth. My breasts hurt from the avid exploration by three pairs of hands. My pelvis hurt from being buffeted by three dark-haired heads, and most of all my back hurt from its contact with the hard, uneven, splinter-riddled table. I felt as though I'd been trampled by a herd of elephants.

I was appalled at my own behaviour, by the abandoned noises I'd been making, and most of all I was appalled by how close I had come to losing my virginity.

Looking back on the event I can now cynically wish the boys had gone the whole way. But at the time my reaction was disgust at myself. Because of my total loss of self-control I had, I felt, missed by only a whisker a fate worse than death. But that was not all. In retrospect, I could now see that this debauchery was the trigger for a subsequent act of mine that was quite unforgivable. That in turn must have given me a permanent guilt complex. As a result my over-indecent enjoyment of being mauled by three pairs of hands turned out to be very bad psychological conditioning. Sex had become associated in my mind with shame. Had I merely been mildly interested or vaguely aroused I would probably have returned to England determined to find out more about sex, and then, over the next couple of years, I might have turned into a normal woman, with normal manageable urges. As it was, that little orgy preceded a betrayal I could not forgive myself for. My determination that such depravity must never happen again had all the strength and the permanence of a religious conversion.

And now here I was, married to Sir Peter Easton, the most eligible man in Britain, with not just permission to have sex but even, one might argue, an obligation and a duty to put it regularly his way and enjoy it. But now I was *Lady* Sarah. That made things a hundred times worse. A lady simply does not slip into the abyss of abandonment into which I had plunged at Lindos, especially if the servants are probably listening.

So perhaps that was the explanation I had been searching for; my fear of releasing the latent slut within me was what made me tremble so uncontrollably, and was what had so far prevented my acceptance of Peter's embrace.

# Chapter Eight

The dishes were put away, the kitchen was spick and span. I could have rejoined the other guests to try and find out what one actually did during a normal day at Sister Murdock's House of Correction. But no one was bugging me so I sat sipping a coffee, watching the gardener at work in the distance. He was forking compost or manure onto the flowerbeds and he had taken his shirt off. I could see his lean back was quite as sun-bronzed as mine, though I could be sure his tan had been acquired much more cheaply.

At last he stuck his fork in the earth, stretched, picked up his bits and pieces and set off for the far corner of the house. I waited until he disappeared from view and then I crept cautiously along the corridors, on the lookout for Sister Murdock, till I found the door of the room Astrud had described. I tried the handle but it was locked. So I knocked.

'Who's there?' came a startled grunt.

'My name's Sarah,' I called, my voice hushed. 'I'm one of the guests. I want to talk to you.'

There was a puzzled pause, then, 'Just a minute.'

I heard him rummaging about inside, and then the door opened. He had put a mask on, a dog's head with floppy ears. What a truly peculiar place Sister Murdock ran!

'Well?' he snapped.

His hairy chest was partly covered only by an old moth-eaten jacket, he was still wearing his wellington boots, and they and his coarse grey trousers smelled of manure. He was generally pretty distasteful. The gruff tone of his question didn't bode too well, either.

'I – I was hoping you might help me escape from the house,' I blurted, my plan for discretion completely flying out of my head.

'More'n my job's worth.' He immediately started to push the door closed, herding me out.

'No, no, I'll pay you,' I blustered.

'You got money?' He spoke with a country accent, very bluntly. But at least he was interested.

'Yes,' I said. 'I have money.'

'Show me,' he grunted.

'I don't have it with me – I'll give you a cheque.' Straight away I knew how silly that sounded.

'A cheque?' he scoffed. 'What bloody use is a cheque to me?'

'A hundred pounds?' I tempted.

'Cash?'

'No,' I said, shaking my head, 'I don't have the cash. I just told you. It'll have to be a cheque.'

He simply shook his head dismissively.

'Two hundred pounds, then?' I tried.

'You willing to pay two hundred pounds to get out o' here?' he asked.

'Yes, yes,' I said, a little too eagerly.

'Bloody 'ell.' He scratched his whiskered chin. 'Must be desperate. You can suck my dick, then.'

I had imagined that last bit, surely!

'What... what did you say?' I stammered.

'I'll let you out if'n you suck my dick,' he repeated.

'Don't be preposterous!' I snapped indignantly.

He said nothing, but I could see his eyes through the holes in the mask and he was staring at me most strangely. Damn it! Why couldn't I have been ugly? Or do men like being sucked off by ugly girls, too?

'No,' I said firmly.

'You want to get out of here, you suck my dick,' he repeated uncompromisingly.

Obviously it was unthinkable. He must see that.

'Five hundred pounds,' I offered.

'Okay,' he agreed.

What a relief. 'You'll let me out for five hundred pounds?'

'Yeah,' he confirmed. 'But you gotta suck my dick as well.'

I gave a little scream of frustration. 'You stupid man!'

'I'm not stupid,' he said indignantly. 'It's you what wants to pay five hundred pound to get out of a house you paid more'n a thousand to get in,' he pointed out with infuriating logic.

I stared at him, my hands set on my hips. This man, looked like a dog and smelled like a pig. And he expected me to perform an utterly degrading act for his pleasure. Just to unlock the door for me.

Well, I couldn't.

Could I?

There is something seriously wrong with me. Every time when confronted by an impossibly indecent proposal its sheer impossibility somehow made me want to do it. That familiar bubbly feeling was back in my stomach. That sharp image of what I might look like appeared in my brain; my beautiful innocent face, eyes closed, mouth full and lips stretched around an erect staff, the eventual spurt of unspeakable fluid on my tongue. No, no, no, I told myself. I couldn't do it. It was worse even than what I'd done with Astrud.

There! I had used that one irrefutable argument again. I had been perversely proud of my submission to Astrud because I felt I'd sunk as low as I possibly could and yet come through unscathed. Now I was faced with an even deeper pit into which to lower myself. Therefore it followed that I *must* do it. Otherwise I would have admitted to myself that I was a coward and a prude.

'All right,' I conceded hoarsely, and when I heard the words come out I had the greatest difficulty believing I had really said them.

Without further ceremony he unzipped his grubby trousers. I knelt on the floor in front of him and pulled the fat but still limp object into my mouth.

Memories of Lindos flashed before my eyes. I started moving my head tentatively, but my rustic tyrant wasn't satisfied. He grabbed it firmly between his shovel-like hands and worked it back and forth in long, steady strokes. I hadn't bargained for this, I thought. What does he think I am? An inflatable Japanese doll?

I could have tried to push his hands away but I didn't. Suddenly it seemed entirely appropriate that I should be treated no better than a plastic toy. 'The way to a man's heart is through his prick,' one of the girls once said at Westover, deliberately shocking us all. Well, this man's brains were currently concentrated in his prick. I had only to service it to have him in my power.

But then he held my head still.

'Use your tongue,' he directed thickly.

The fellow was an uncouth lout, but with a perverse pleasure I did what he said. I stiffened my tongue to a point and bullied the head of his truncheon with it. I remembered something I'd read in a book on biology at school, that the strange indentation at the base of the head is where the most sensitive nerves are. I stabbed away at that and, lo and behold, the red monster, already almost too huge for my mouth, grew a few more centimetres in girth.

That's showing you, I thought. That'll teach you to boss me around. You're mine and I'll make you beg for it.

The beast in my mouth was now hot and engorged with blood. It was also incredibly hard, its head bulging fit to burst. Visions of myself as the primal female predator flashed through my mind. One bite and my victim would collapse, his blood instantly draining from his body. It was good to have that power, and that strange erotic feeling in my stomach welled up again.

I'm winning, I thought, and I began to pump with my head again, this time faster and further. I heard an odd noise in the room and recognised it as that same moaning I'd heard in the beach hut at Lindos. Sarah realised with embarrassment that there was some woman in there who was getting very worked up over something. She should be ashamed of herself, Sarah thought primly. But Sarah was rapidly fading into the distance. Sally the slut was back and in charge.

There's something so crude and childish about the word, suck. It rhymes with the f-word, of course, but is in some way much less threatening. The f-word is what men do, but sucking is a woman's prerogative. I'm the mover, I thought, the one that's in charge. Now, every time I pulled back from him I sucked as hard as I could, willing him to yield. I was the vampire, possessing my victim, draining him. Give it to me, I thought, I want it. I want you to burst, spilling your manhood, screaming as your life force is drained from you, as you fall back limp and impotent. Samson shorn by Delilah. Romeo castrated by Juliet. Mine.

The explosion came, as it had to. The dog howled as though he had been cornered by the fox in a hunt, and my world was suddenly full of a thick, slightly salty fluid. For some seconds the distended staff continued to pump spurts of love into my mouth. Then the room fell abruptly silent except for the dog's heavy breathing. The arrogant monster in my mouth gradually withdrew into itself and became a shy little boy again. I licked the last few drops of my defeated victim's blood and stood up.

'Okay?' I said.

'Bloody 'ell, that were great,' panted the dog's head.

'Good.' I felt somehow very smug. 'Then let me out.'

He failed to move and my spirits fell.

'I can't do that,' he said.

'Why not? You promised!'

'Maybe I lied,' he sneered. 'Here's the thing. If you's willin' to pay five hundred pound to get away only a day after you's arrived, then just think how much more you'll be willin' to pay tomorrow, when you knows what this place is really like.'

'You bastard,' I spat.

'I know, but my wife'd never forgive me if I let you off so easy. Come back same time tomorrow afternoon. Then I'll set you free. I promise.'

With that he was gone, locking the outer door behind him, and I had debased myself for nothing. I suddenly felt sick of the whole silly business, just as I had after the holiday at Lindos. It would have been easy to blame that afternoon's fiasco on the gardener, but I knew it wasn't that simple. My trouble was that I lost all sense of proportion once I got involved in sex. At the time I felt enormously curious, driven on to commit whatever grossness presented itself by a sense of adventure and investigation, not simple lust.

But afterwards I saw myself for the slut I was, ashamed that I was so eager to perform these monstrosities for their own sake.

I tried to remember that I was now a respectable married woman. Why was I so inconsistent? How could I have allowed myself to service the gardener in such a crude way, yet I hadn't had the courage to act like that while with Peter? It was the anonymity, I supposed. With Peter, whatever I did I would have to live with – it would be a shared knowledge that neither of us could deny. With a stranger, well it was just a matter of walking away, wasn't it?

With Tassos, for instance. Except of course then Megan had been aware that something pretty extreme had been going on.

After I'd finished my moaning and groaning in the beach store with Tassos and the other two boys I found the thong, put it on again, and ran straight down into the sea. My back was covered in dust, there was sand and wood shavings in my hair, and my bottom sported quite a few scratches from the splinters on the table. The thong covered nothing and I was acutely aware that the clear imprint of the table was visible on my back.

I had never felt so conspicuous as I did as I hurried down the beach, sure that everyone was looking round at the girl who had made all that noise. I ran into the sea as far as my neck and just sat there, trembling. The salt stung my numerous scratches and soon I knew where every little injury I had received was located. Then I stuck my head under, tried to rinse the sand out of my hair, and had a really good cry. I was also emotionally overwrought and I couldn't really believe what I'd done. But all my senses told me it had really happened.

I stayed in the sea for probably more than an hour. I was terrified of going back to see Megan. The longer I stayed there the more appalled I became at the length of time I would have been absent. And then it occurred to me that she might have seen me run out of the hut and down to the sea and have been watching me ever since, wondering what I was doing. Well, it was no good pretending nothing had taken place. I would have to admit that something pretty dreadful had happened in the hut, but I needn't, of course, admit the whole shocking truth.

When I at last went back to my beach towel Megan sat up, eyes glinting with anger, and swore at me.

'What in Christ's name have you been up to, you whore?' she said venomously.

I picked up the half-empty can of Gini and drained it gratefully. It tasted like hot rancid urine. I lay down on my back, trying to hide the scratches.

'Not so loud,' I muttered in a stage whisper. 'Everyone can hear.'

'Did you sleep with that lad?' she accused vehemently.

I reflected that 'sleep with' is a fairly meaningless expression.

'He's older than he looks,' I said. 'Yes, I did. I didn't really mean to but things got out of hand.'

She turned away huffily. 'Then I hope you'll find somewhere else to sleep tonight because you're certainly not sharing with me.'

And that was the end of our conversation for the day.

I found and paid for a beach umbrella, and curled up under it out of the sun.

When the sun began to get low Megan collected her things. I picked up mine and followed her at a distance, like a puppy. She would probably have locked me out of our room but by great good fortune I had the key, so instead she had to wait for me to let her in.

'Don't be beastly to me, Megan,' I pleaded. 'I'm at the end of my tether. I didn't mean it to happen.'

'You followed him up the beach gaily enough, thrusting your tits at him,' she accused.

'I know,' I admitted shamefully. 'It was this stupid thong. It made me feel randy. I can't explain it. You made me wear it and once I had it on I wanted to behave like a tart.'

'Did he take it off?' she asked, mellowing just a little.

'Yes, of course,' I said.

'What do you mean "of course"? Why didn't you scream?'

'Megan, I wanted him to,' I tried to explain. 'You know? I didn't *mean* him to do it, but I *wanted* him to do it.'

'I don't know what you're talking about,' she said huffily.

'I'm seventeen,' I tried to explain. 'It was time I lost my virginity. That's what I kept thinking.'

'To a Greek schoolboy?' she scoffed.

'Believe me, he's not a schoolboy,' I assured her. 'I'm

sure he's over sixteen, maybe even older than me. I don't know.'

'Do you… do you mean he's fully developed?' she asked inquisitively.

'How should I know?' I protested. 'I've never done it before.'

'Well, I hope you're pleased with yourself.'

'I'm not,' I declared. 'I'm ashamed. But I had to do it, to see what it's like.'

'And what *is* it like?' she asked, with heavy irony.

'I can't remember,' I lied. 'It just happened.'

'Did it hurt?'

'Yes.'

'A lot?'

'Yes, I think so. I can't remember. It certainly hurts now.'

'Let me have a look,' she said, mellowing again. 'Go on, take a shower.'

So that's what I did, and I must say the hot water was a great relief. Megan followed me in as I started to wash.

'Let me do that,' she said, undressing. She took the flannel from me. 'Oh, you poor darling, you're covered in bruises,' she cooed maternally.

'I know.'

'He's a monster!' she snapped. 'We'll report him to the police.'

'We can't do that,' I said. 'He was just a little overeager.'

'A little?'

'I was lying on a wooden table.'

'What?' she said, aghast. 'How disgusting. Did he kiss you?'

'Yes.'

'On the mouth?'

'Well, no.' Why was I being so honest?

'Where then?' she probed.

I didn't know what to say.

'Did he kiss you... you know... down there?'

'Yes,' I admitted.

'That's disgraceful,' she said, screwing up her face.

'Well so did you,' I pointed out. 'Last night.'

Oops! I was supposed to have been asleep. Megan blushed fiercely.

'That's different,' she mumbled. 'We're girls.'

There was an uncomfortable pause.

'You won't expect me to kiss you there again, will you?' she said haughtily. 'Not after he's had his thing in it?'

'I'm sorry,' I apologised, 'I wasn't thinking.'

But the odd thing was that now she'd said she wouldn't do it she became obsessed with the idea. First she dabbed around with the flannel. Then she made me turn around with my back to her and bend over. Expressing great concern she gently touched my pouting sex.

'It's so red and sore,' she whispered.

'Men are such beasts,' I said, fishing for sympathy.

'Yes, aren't they,' she agreed. 'I don't understand why nature makes it so difficult. Why the girl has to suffer so much.'

'That was what made it exciting.' I began to fantasise. 'Megan, it was like there was something *serious* happening to me at last. It wasn't just a finger, or a candle, it was the real thing; fat and ferocious.'

She kissed me, just where she said she never would again.

'How big was it?' she whispered, curiosity getting the better of her.

One lie leads to another, I suppose.

'I don't know, do I?' I fudged. 'It just felt huge, like it was a fist or something.'

'Ugh, no. You poor dear.' Her tongue began to tickle the tender flesh.

'Thank you, Megan, that feels wonderful,' I sighed.

Amazing. Only the night before I'd had to pretend to be asleep because I was too ashamed to admit I was letting her do it. Now I was thanking her! Thing was, I'd found one of my sexual images to toy with. I saw the three lads, smoking and laughing, standing beside the table while Megan fussed and fretted over me. When she was done she handed me back to them and they had their way with me, savagely and casually, while she stood watching, gasping with pain each time I did. Then, when they'd finished with me and needed time to recuperate, she washed me down lovingly again, ready for the whole cycle to repeat itself.

The thing that really turned me on about this was that it was my body that was the central attraction. That's what they all wanted, Megan and the boys. I wasn't obliged to offer anything in return, I simply had to allow them to do what they wanted with it. Aroused by this fantasy, and before I knew what was happening, I was gasping and groaning with passion, pushing my buttocks against Megan's face, begging her to delve ever deeper. And through the open window once again the streets of Lindos rang with the sounds of my excitement. I could imagine the passers-by nodding to each other, 'Oh that'll be the girl in the thong again. She's a noisy one, and no mistake!'

But I didn't care.

The shower ran cold as the solar tank emptied, but I

didn't care. Megan had won me back from the awful Tassos, and she didn't care. I grunted and groaned and made a thorough slut of myself. But I still didn't care.

Megan and I were friends again.

# Chapter Nine

After being cheated by the gardener I spent the rest of the afternoon in my room reading a book. I'd no doubt Astrud and the girls were having a fine time somewhere, setting each other forfeits, but I was so annoyed at being duped that I couldn't face anyone else.

At the back of my mind was the knowledge that I had yet another decision to make. Dinner was at six o'clock. The last there would be punished. The ceremonial paddle, SM had said, though I still had a feeling she was bluffing.

A coward would go down at about five-thirty, or maybe even earlier, to be sure of escaping her wrath. But I was determined not to appear to be a coward by adopting such a sissy tactic. Sister M had my number in her book. Heavy sarcasm would come my way if I was a good girl and arrived early. On the other hand, heavy tribulation might be mine if I deliberately arrived late.

To check things out I actually walked past the door of the dining room just after five-thirty. The table was already nearly full, but I could, if I'd gone in then, have avoided being last. Dammit, I thought, I wouldn't be one of the herd. It was ridiculous to sit down for a meal half an hour early. I'd go in my own good time, whatever the cost.

I have to admit that I found such defiance quite thrilling; a bit like walking a tightrope. My fertile imagination already visualised me bending over to touch my toes while 'teacher' applied her version of the cane. I saw myself stand up again, proud and tall, no murmur escaping my lips, shaming Sister Murdock by my dignified disregard for her unlawful punishment.

That was Sarah playing the part of being proud and regal, contemptuous of Sister Murdock's methods, which were by any standards quite indefensible in a civilised society. But Sally had a different reason for courting such chastisement. I had been at Athelstan Hall for just twenty-four hours and my behaviour had so far been anything but proud and regal. It had been every bit as indefensible as Sister Murdock's, and quite a lot more bizarre. What had got into me? It was as if some dam had burst, after the strain of the marriage and the first couple of weeks as Lady Sarah. So Sally genuinely felt she deserved some fairly serious punishment, and a strange moist feeling inside me, while not welcoming any actual pain, still welcomed the significance of such pain. If Sister Murdock really did hit me then I could go home to Peter in the knowledge that I had paid for my indiscretions and, thank heavens, I would have some major talking-point which would conveniently circumvent any questions about what I had really been doing at Athelstan Hall.

I was deep in this reverie of self-pity, self-admiration, and self-admonishment when someone tugged at my elbow. It was Katerina, the secretary.

'It's lucky I found you, Lady Sarah,' she said. 'Your husband's on the phone from Japan. Will you take the call in my office, please?'

I jerked to full awareness. Peter had phoned, just as he'd promised. But what was I to tell him? Well obviously that I wanted him to get me out of the place, right away. After all, only a couple of hours earlier I'd subjected myself to a degrading sexual act with a man smelling of dung, just so I could escape.

I picked up the phone.

'Peter?' I said. 'How was your trip?'

'Dreadful,' came the reply. 'I've barely closed my eyes since I left you. I'm hopeless at sleeping on planes.'

'Cancel your meeting and go to bed now,' I suggested.

'I can't,' he said wearily. 'How about you, Sarah? How's Athelstan Hall? Is it just a money-spinning charade?'

I noticed that Katerina was still within earshot, and she was plainly fascinated by this mundane conversation between the rich and famous.

'Strange is the best word for it,' I said. 'It's not a bit like I expected. The lady that runs it says we're here to broaden our minds.'

'Sister Murdock? Jessica spoke to her over the phone. Is she really a nun?'

'I rather doubt it, though she dresses like one,' I said. 'I've got an odd feeling the whole place is a black joke.'

'A joke?' he said. 'What do you mean?'

'Well, it's like something out of the middle-ages,' I told him.

Bugger Katerina. She could tell Sister Murdock what I'd said if she wanted to. Besides, they'd had me washing dishes all morning.

'Really? Well don't stay there then. I'll give Kendrick a ring now and tell him to get down there and pick you up tonight.'

Kendrick was our chauffeur. So all I had to say was 'yes', and he'd be there in a couple of hours. Sister Murdock could hardly hold me against my will if there was a driver outside waiting for me.

'No,' I said. 'I'll stick it for another day. Maybe it'll get better.'

'Very well, if you're sure,' he said. 'Look pet, I really have had an exhausting trip and I'm totally drained. I'll ring you same time tomorrow.'

So we said our goodbyes and he rung off. I was quite unable to explain my own behaviour. 'Strange' was how I'd described Athelstan Hall. Wasn't that perhaps a trifle weak for a place where the men wore weird masks? Where they were instructed to perform any service required of them? Where the guests were punished by doing the cooking? I suddenly flushed hot with embarrassment as I visualised myself under the shower with Astrud. This was a lunatic asylum, run by a sado-masochistic harridan, and I was unfortunately a worthy inmate.

And had I already been legally unfaithful to Peter? I could not recall any words in the marriage service that had specifically declared cock sucking off limits. But the *Sunday Globe* would probably nevertheless interpret it in a most unfavourable light.

Katerina was still staring at me. I looked at my watch. Five-fifty. Bags of time.

'Can I call my mother?' I asked.

'Of course,' Katerina said. 'Give me the number and I'll connect you.'

So there I was waffling on to my mum, describing the delphiniums in the garden, but not the gardener, the delectable wine at dinner, but not the getting drunk, my room on the second floor, but not the shower stall along the landing.

As a result of my second call it was exactly two minutes past six when I walked proudly into the dining room and sat down in the last available place.

Wide eyes stared at me aghast. I was the bad girl of the class.

Sister Murdock had apparently managed to acquire the services of a new domestic, and we were treated to an excellent meal; Belgian pâté, cold salmon, medallions of pork in a piquant mustard sauce, and lemon sorbet. And this time a sparkling wine, the origin eluding me.

Conversation was pleasant but non-committal; I think the forthcoming forfeit was on everyone's mind, not just mine. I caught what I took to be several admiring glances from the other girls that I should now appear so calm, and that I should so brazenly have stood up against Sister Murdock's tyranny.

But my calmness was only skin deep. Inside I was trembling like a child. I recalled one of my escapades at Westover when I had crept into the kitchen and filled the sugar jar with salt, which the half-witted cook subsequently used in the staff's peach crumble. As a result I had been hauled up before the headmistress for a blistering reprimand that left me crying and shaken. But on that occasion I had known that corporal punishment was not allowed. Whereas in this madhouse anything seemed possible. Sister Murdock couldn't really beat me, could she…?

At seven-thirty precisely Sister Murdock clapped her hands for silence and the three remaining men took their places at the corners of the room, clad exactly as they had been the previous evening.

'Well, ladies, I hope you enjoyed your meal,' she said. 'This is Jacqueline,' she waved towards the new cook-cum-waitress, 'and I'm sure you'll agree she has done a first-rate job.'

There was a ripple of applause.

'I should like to publicly thank Lady Sarah for the lunch, earlier today. I am sure none of us could have done better. Unfortunately, Lady Sarah has rather blotted her copybook by being last down to dinner for the second day running. What do you have to say for yourself, my dear?'

I was scared, but I shrugged defiantly. 'Someone has to be last,' I said.

'Of course,' the woman agreed. 'But that someone need not be you. I believe you have deliberately invited the requisite punishment, which is on the second day, as I warned you, physical.'

She pointed to the paddle over the mantelpiece.

'Tonight I shall administer just a single stroke,' she went on. 'Tomorrow, for whoever is last, there will be two strokes. On Wednesday I shall use four and on Thursday, our last evening together, a full six of the best.'

So she really meant it! I was suddenly almost overwhelmed by the fear that wafted over me like a cold draught. The little child was back and desperate to run away. I could not imagine how, a short while before, I had found the idea of being beaten exciting. I could hear my own breathing, nervous and unsteady.

Then suddenly Sally the slut regained control, and the telltale moisture had already gathered between my legs and excitement overwhelmed fear.

I knew I had to make an important decision. Should I accept the punishment meekly, or should I resist? There was something very beguiling about the vision of me bending over willingly to be spanked – the ritual victim laying her head on the block. But on the other hand, I wanted to make Sister Murdock work for her petty victory. After all, she had totally overstepped the mark. This was not some antiquated public school where caning was a way of life. This was the real world where even a registered penal institution could no longer use corporal punishment. I took a deep breath and prepared to play the part of Lady Sarah.

'I'm afraid I'm not going to agree to your entirely unjustified forfeit,' I announced. 'I'm going to my room.'

With that I got up haughtily and turned away. Sarah was back in control, but even she could sense that the evening would be a terrible anti-climax if Sister Murdock lamely gave in.

'But you don't have that option,' the woman said coldly.

I turned and faced her, blood singing in my head. I reminded myself that I was Sir Peter Easton's wife, and not the trembling twelve-year-old I felt.

'Most certainly I do,' I countered. 'This is still a free country, I hope. If you lay so much as a finger on me I shall take you to court. Is that clear?'

'Bravely said,' she mocked. 'Unfortunately, you are not out and at large in this free country. You are here, a captive inside Athelstan Hall, a house of correction. Submission, as I have already warned you, is one of the major subjects on the curriculum. You don't seem ready yet to accept the indignity of being beaten. For that is all it is. No physical harm will come to you. It may even surprise you to know that you will be the last of this week's guests to have to submit to corporal punishment. The others have all been chastised for one reason or another earlier today, when you were either otherwise engaged, or perhaps deliberately avoiding us.'

'I don't believe you,' I gasped, utterly deflated.

'Amarinda, would you stand up, please,' the ogre asked assuredly.

The girl with Indian features got gingerly to her feet. She was a little plump, with huge dark eyes and thick black hair like a waterfall down her back.

'Amarinda was brought here by two of her brothers,' the woman explained. 'She has refused to marry the suitor of her father's choice, claiming she is in love with an English boy. I must say that personally I have a great deal of sympathy for her plight. However, I agreed to help her family persuade her that parents know best. Her punishment level has already been high, and it will continue so throughout the week. Amarinda, would you be so good as to show Lady Sarah your bottom?'

The girl obediently unwound her red and gold sari to reveal a strangely incongruous pair of modern briefs. She lowered them and turned to display herself to me. Her buttocks were already a savage red under the olive of her skin, and several separate weals were visible.

I gasped. 'You cruel beast!' I said angrily to Sister Murdock.

'Yes, yes, I am just that,' she acknowledged. 'But that does not alter the fact that you are going to have to accept your punishment. We'd all far prefer it to be willingly. But force can be used, if that's what you want. Now would you please lean over the table.'

'Never!' I refused petulantly.

The Sarah part of me was thinking like a lawyer; there were witnesses, she said. But the Sally part of me, the ever-present slut, was wondering exactly how the experience would feel, to be spanked in a sexually degrading way.

In any event, it looked as if both halves of me were going to have their wishes granted. At a sign from the old witch, Lance and Pearce were at my elbows.

They dragged me, struggling but not screaming, over to the end of the table and pulled me face down over it. I felt a hand lift my skirt and another pull down my briefs.

'Help me, someone,' I pleaded, now genuinely horrified. But the other girls, even Astrud, stared at me with uncertainty in their eyes.

'Stop fighting,' murmured Amarinda. 'It'll be easier.'

Sister Murdock had retrieved the paddle from above the fireplace. But she still overheard Amarinda. 'Did you say something?' she snarled.

Amarinda cringed away. 'I just told her to stop fighting,' she defended herself.

'You should know better than to speak to an inmate who's being punished,' the woman hissed. 'Assume the chastisement position.'

The poor girl did exactly as she was told, bending over to touch her toes without hesitation. The paddle flashed out and there was a sharp, greedy smack. She jerked forward both from pain and from the sheer force of the clout. The air rushed from her throat and tears sprang to her eyes. Weeping softly, she resumed her place at the long table even more gingerly than she had vacated it.

I was held down between the two lines of seated girls. I knew the blow would fall soon and I knew they were all watching my eyes to see how I would take it. I struggled again, kicking out in the hope I might catch Sister Murdock.

'Help them hold her down, girls,' she snapped crossly.

'Lance, Pearce, grab her ankles.'

All the girls did as she commanded, pinning my shoulders and arms to the table. But several of them, Astrud included, tried to give my fingers an encouraging squeeze. Male hands gripped my ankles and knees, and I prepared myself for the onslaught.

But Sister Murdock obviously saw some merit in letting me sweat. She walked round to the opposite side of the table where I could see her and stood there, swinging the paddle against her hand with evident relish. She leaned over and smiled in my face.

'I think you've had this coming for a little while, Lady Sarah,' she said menacingly.

Then she disappeared from view. There was complete silence in the room. They were all waiting for the paddle to fall and they were all waiting for my scream. Whatever happened I must deny them that pleasure.

I heard the blow before I felt it. It was a crisp crack, almost like a stick breaking. I had time to think that it really wasn't so bad, before the shock hit me. It's not easy to describe the pain but I know it was green in colour. This huge wash of liquid agony swept over me, clawing at my feet, my calves, my shoulders, my thighs, my breasts, my belly.

But mostly my buttocks.

For a moment I thought my dinner was going to appear over the table in front of me.

But somehow I held it down. However, I could not hold back the sharp salty tears that sprang spontaneously to my eyes. Nor could I suppress the enormous rush of air that was expelled from my lungs. But I did manage not to cry out.

Sister Murdock again appeared in front of me and leaned forward, a smug grin on her face. 'You'll thank me for this later,' she gloated.

In reply I spat at her.

I was so caught up in my indignant playacting that I did it as if it were called for by the scene I was playing. It's something you often see in films and it's something I've always thought disgusting, something I would never do. But then I'd never been in such a highly charged situation before.

'Hold her down,' Sister Murdock commanded, wiping her face.

She disappeared again and immediately a second blow fell, far more painful than the first, finding sore, bruised flesh. My whole body jerked convulsively and I lay there, still pinioned, my breath sawing erratically through my clenched teeth. My chest heaved miserably. I had not known or imagined that agony could feel so fierce and hot. There was no help from the other girls and indeed, from the corner of my eye I noticed that Freya, the girl with the glasses, was obviously enjoying the spectacle. She licked her lips hungrily and her eyes sparkled with anticipation. But for me the playacting was over and I lay there, dreading what I knew must happen next.

Sister Murdock's face reappeared and moved slowly to within a couple of inches of mine. 'That was very brave, Lady Sarah,' she hissed. 'I congratulate you. You now have another chance to express your hatred.'

I knew I must do it, of course, no matter what it cost me. In fact, it was only the pain that must follow that made the defiance worthwhile. But my mouth felt so dry, almost as if my own body were conspiring against me. I swallowed hard a couple of times and at last felt the saliva coming back. I gathered up what I could – and that was pitifully little – and expelled it full against her face, so close to mine.

There, I'd done it!

But now I had to grimly await my fate. And strangely, despite the awful tension of the situation, I had the detachment to notice that Sister Murdock was wearing make-up, which had smudged when she wiped her face. Good God, I thought, she must be even older than she looked, a dry worn out stick with no way to get her kicks other than to torture younger, more attractive women.

For it was torture, I had no doubt. Maybe a knife under the fingernails, or a beating on the soles of the feet, or a red-hot needle piercing one's nipple might be far more harmful, but I found it difficult, right then, to imagine that it could be more painful.

The third blow was finally too much for me. I had invited it but I could not overcome it. A despairing cry burst from my lips and from deep down in my throat. A similar gasp escaped Freya's throat and she closed her eyes in fulfilment. Too exhausted to be angry, a wave of giddiness swept over me and for a minute I thought I would pass out.

'Let her up,' Sister Murdock said.

I straightened myself cautiously and felt hands rearranging my clothing.

'You give up, then?' I managed, though it came out little better than a croak.

'Yes, I give up,' she conceded. 'You have more spirit than I gave you credit for. You win. Until tomorrow.'

# Chapter Ten

I limped stiffly but with what I hoped was dignity from the dining room, and climbed wearily up the stairs. I heard a step behind me. It was Amarinda.

'Come back to my room,' she said. 'I have something that will help you.'

I didn't have the strength to argue. I wanted to cry but the tears wouldn't come. It seemed I was all dried up. How could I have been so silly as to willingly consign myself to such a hellhole? Amarinda's parents had forced her to attend. At least she had the comfort of knowing the situation was not her fault. But I had no one to blame but myself, and I had even passed up the opportunity to escape, offered by Peter's call.

'Lie down on your stomach,' she said, when we were in the security of her room. 'I have some lotion.'

I did not imagine for a moment any ointment or salve would have the slightest effect, but it was nice that someone felt sorry for me. She was incredibly careful, undressing me completely, sliding my clothes out from under me when I seemed to have lost the strength to help. And wonder upon wonders, the lotion was marvellous. In seconds the agony had dimmed to a burning glow, which was not only bearable but almost, in some strange way, enjoyable.

'It's got some sort of anaesthetic in it,' she explained.

'You brought it with you?' I asked, intrigued.

'Yes,' she said. 'I knew I was in for it. My mother and father had been discussing sending me here for months.'

She handed me the bottle.

'Will you do me now, Lady Sarah?' she asked sweetly.

'Of course,' I said, happy to oblige the sweet girl who'd helped me. 'And it's Sally, by the way.'

She began to undress, and as her body was slowly revealed from under the yards of silk encasing it, I came to realise what an alluring shape she was. It was as if she'd stepped out of one of those erotic Hindu wall paintings.

Although you wouldn't describe her as fat, she had rounded hips like a fertility goddess. Her belly was firm but ripe. I didn't get much of a look at her breasts because she immediately lay down on her front, but I could tell they were large.

I used the lotion sparingly, having already appreciated its value. My fingers worked it ever so lightly into the skin of her tender buttocks, incongruously pink against the brown of the rest of her body.

She sighed contentedly. 'That's so much better, Sally.'

'Was it true, what Sister Murdock said about you?' I asked.

'More or less,' she admitted. 'The boy she referred to, Terry, is not a Hindu. To my parents that makes him one of the untouchables.'

'But you're living in Britain now,' I pointed out. 'You have the right to choose your own husband, Amarinda. How old are you?'

'Nineteen,' she said.

'There you are. Simply marry Terry when you get out of here. They can't stop you. I'll help you, if they try.'

She shrugged. 'But I don't want to marry Terry,' she

disclosed.

I was confused. 'Why not?'

'Because he's a shit,' she said with feeling, catching me by surprise. 'I'd be better off married to Runji – their choice.' She laughed at the bewilderment on my face. 'Look, I'd better tell you the whole story. Then you won't blame my parents so much.'

She rolled onto her side, facing me, and I had to suppress a gasp as her breasts came into view. Now, mine are neatly generous in size and shape, but hers were *large*. She was, in truth, a voluptuous sight, and I had no doubt most men – if not all men – would willingly have died for a night in her arms.

'Um, are you a virgin?' I asked.

It seemed unlikely that a girl as blatantly and gratuitously sexy as she, could have survived into her late teens without succumbing to the begging and blandishments of at least a platoon of men. But she nodded.

'Yes, but I can't claim to be a 'good' girl, if that's what you're thinking.'

I was puzzled. 'What do you mean?' I probed.

'I'll have to tell you about my first evening with Terry,' she confided. 'He's a pop star, or at least he thinks he is. His group, *Sex on a Stick*, has made a couple of records, although any group can do that if they're willing to foot the bill.

'But that's how I met him, when he was playing at the local youth club in Brixton where I'd gone with my brothers, Kumar and Rajid. Terry saw me dancing – goodness knows I was sedate enough – but he must have had the smarts to realise that there was an unusually large bosom hidden under my sari.

'When the gig finished he begged me to go with him. He said they were going to a "smart club" up in town and that the night had "only just started", even though it was after midnight. I waited till the group had packed up all their gear and then I slipped away from my brothers. But of course they were bound to guess I'd gone with Terry. After all, they'd seen me talking to him.

'We went up to the West End of London but the smart club turned out to be nothing but a sleazy strip joint. I was pretty shocked, but by then I was stuck with the group, having no idea how to get home. The way the club worked was they tried to get girls to come up out of the audience to dance on the stage.

'I reckon they were just paid strippers really, but they made it look as if it was spontaneous. A couple of the girls who went round with Terry's band went up but they were pretty ordinary. Of course Terry wanted me to go up, too. I mean, I knew it was out of the question. But suddenly they were all looking at me, chanting, begging me to strip. And I found I really wanted to. I couldn't understand why, but I knew I wanted to shock them. They all thought I was an innocent Indian girl from a very strict background – which was true – and that's why they wanted me to strip. I knew that when I got down to it I was sexier than they'd ever have imagined, far, far sexier than any of the slags that had been up on the stage so far.'

I listened to her, completely caught up in her story. For a moment I forgot I was Lady Sarah Easton and wondered whether I could nip up to London sometime and pretend to be a stripper, just for the fun of it. But someone would recognise me. So that thrill was forever unattainable.

'But you didn't really strip, did you, Amarinda?' I asked.

She paused, and nodded sadly. 'Yes, I'm afraid I did. The thing was, I couldn't just walk away. They'd all think how weedy I was. Whereas I knew if I did what they wanted they'd all fall for me. Then I'd walk away, leaving them with their mouths hanging open. It would be a strange revenge – serve them right for having shouted for it.'

Without thinking what I was doing I reached out and felt one of her breasts. It was like soft dusky oil, running through my fingers. I pressed the nipple, firm and angry, staring at me like a huge eye. 'They are truly amazing,' I murmured.

'Don't I know it,' she said. 'I've had to live with them. The glances in the changing rooms at school – some envious, some disgusted. But no man had ever seen them.

'That was the thing, Sally. If you're an innocent girl you know men are supposed to be turned on by breasts, but you've no idea how much. It seemed it would be so easy. All I had to do was climb up there on the catwalk, take off my clothes, and then watch the reaction. I'd find out at last. So I did. Before I knew it I was unwinding my sari, looking down at all those faces, trying to understand what it was they felt.

'And the funny thing was, I wasn't even nervous when I started. I thought there was no one in the club who could possibly know me, and after it was over I would simply disappear back into oblivion. But I hadn't got very far before I realised the audience reaction was quite beyond anything I could have expected, and way beyond anything I could understand. It was their faces, you see. They were all shouting as well, but to tell you the truth I'd gone into a sort of state of shock and I couldn't pick out any of the words any more. But I could understand their faces; hot, sweaty, mouths open, some sober, some drunk, but all wanting me. No, wanting is too weak a word. They were all lusting for me with an intensity that seems hard to believe now, in the quiet of this room.

'That's when I started to get nervous. If they all want me that much, I thought, why didn't someone start the rush? I could visualise them all over me, fighting, clawing, mad with passion. I'd die long before the police could get there, I knew.

'But funnily enough, they all behaved themselves. No one even tried to reach out and touch me. They realised that I was what I appeared to be; a genuinely innocent girl from an incredibly strict upbringing, who had suddenly and magically lost her restraint. I think they felt they were lucky to see what I had to offer and they didn't want to break the spell.

'Anyway, when I think back on it I realise how utterly pathetic my strip was. There was some sort of music thundering away in the background but I couldn't take it in. I couldn't dance, or move, or smile, or anything. I just stood there, undressing slowly, as if I was in my own bedroom.

'Well, apparently you're not supposed to be completely nude, but I didn't realise that. So I even took my panties off. Then I just stood there, numb, while they all roared their approval. I remember one guy in particular, right up under the catwalk. He was actually dribbling. His mouth hung open and the saliva was running out of the corner of it. Can you imagine how that made me feel?'

She fell silent, drinking in the memory.

'How did you get off the stage?' I prompted quietly.

'Oh, that was awful,' she went on. 'If only I'd made a

run for it as soon as I'd taken my bra off. Then I might have disappeared back into the crowd, incognito. But I must have been up there for two or three minutes after that, not knowing what to do. And during that time my brothers came into the club and saw me.'

'Your brothers?' I gasped. 'But how—?'

'I still can't believe how unlucky I was,' she continued, barely hearing me. 'When I disappeared from the youth club they guessed I'd gone off with the group. They asked around and found someone who said Terry had told them he was going up to Soho. So they followed in their car. When they got to the West End they simply drove round till they saw the band's parked van. They barged into all the nearby clubs until, as luck would have it, they arrived just in time to see me naked and to hear the crowd.

'Well, they bundled me off the stage, wrapped me in a jacket, and pushed me outside. Luckily it was obvious that they were my brothers and that they were appalled at what they'd found, otherwise they might have started the stampede I was so afraid of.'

'I guess you had a tough time when you got home,' I said.

'Well what do you think?' she snorted. 'The roof fell in on me. My parents couldn't or wouldn't believe it, but the evidence was unarguable – I had arrived back home without any of the clothes I went out in.

'I was locked up in my room for days on end, nothing to eat but bread and water. And my father beat me. Every day for a week.' She gave a hollow laugh. 'This place is a doddle compared to my own home.'

'Look, Amarinda,' I ventured, 'I can see that you behaved badly and I know you've been brought up to obey your parents. But you're old enough to make up your own mind. They can't force you to marry Runji, and they certainly have no right to send you here, telling Sister Murdock to thrash you.'

'No, Sally, you still don't really understand,' she said. 'It's true Terry was so enamoured by what he saw that he kept ringing up, even though my parents screamed insults at him over the phone when he did. But he's not my boyfriend. Never was, never will be. He even tried to come round one evening but my brothers threw him over the garden gate. But so what? I told you, he's a shit. He's a no-hoper, stupid, self-centred, thick as a plank. And what's more, he's ugly. He looks like a water rat. Now Runji is hardworking, well off, truly handsome, kind and considerate, and he thinks the world of me. So who would you choose?'

'The one you love.' I stated what I thought was the obvious.

'What's love got to do with it?' she sneered. 'It's damn hard to fall in love when you can't even touch your suitor, let alone find out what he's like in bed. If Terry hadn't come along I would have happily married Runji. And then I would have easily fallen in love with him and with the children he would have given me. What you've got to understand is that he still knows nothing about my jaunt up to Soho. My family would die rather than let it be known. But if he *did* find out the engagement would be off, like a shot.'

'Now I'm really confused,' I admitted. 'So what's the problem? Why did your parents send you here? Why don't you just agree to marry him?'

'He may not know I've stood on a stage and stripped,

but I do,' she explained. 'It was the most exciting experience of my life. It was a buzz so intense that I don't suppose I'll ever match it again. If I marry Runji then I've *got* to be respectable. And I just can't bear the thought of that, however stupid that makes me. Marriage would write me off to a life of obscurity, even if it were enjoyable obscurity. I'm just an ordinary girl like millions of others. The only thing I have that sets me apart from the majority of them is my body. And there's nothing you can do with a body like this except strip. What a waste if I don't! All I've got to do is lose my dignity and I could be very well off. But I'd also be a total outcast from my family and friends.'

I stared sadly at her, comprehending at last. Once again I realised how easy it had been for me. Whatever happened to me in the future I would always be 'someone', the girl who married Sir Peter Easton. 'I see.' I nodded slowly. 'Then you really do have a problem.'

'Sally, here's the bad bit,' she went on. 'I've actually been back there, to the strip club. My parents couldn't keep me off college forever. Eventually they let me out, saying I'd been ill. I behaved myself for a few days and then I skived off one afternoon, back up to Soho, where I eventually found the place. It's called *The Good Ship Venus*. I told the boss man I'd come back to get my clothes which, to give him credit, he still had. But then he wanted me to strip again. To tell me how it should really be done, he said, the creep. It was only him, the barman, and a cleaner, but it was an audience. I couldn't resist, and it was nearly as good a feeling as the first time.

'He said he'd pay me a thousand pounds a week, for about thirty minutes' work a night. That's the problem.'

I lay there looking at her. I'm not a prude, but I could see horribly clearly that what the man was offering was no good. She might still get a thrill at the beginning, but after a week of stripping three or four times a night it would become just another dreary job. And one that was both dodgy and short-lived.

'Amarinda,' I said slowly, 'I think I've got an idea.'

'An idea for what?' she asked.

'A solution to your problem,' I told her.

'There can be no solution,' she insisted morosely.

'Yes, there can,' I said, yawning. 'I'm going to sleep now and I'll think about it some more in the morning.'

Amarinda switched off the bedside light and pulled my head down to her bosom. It was like being a baby again. I sucked one of her nipples into my mouth and toyed with it until I fell asleep. She didn't seem to mind.

# Chapter Eleven

I woke up the next morning sore and stiff, but comforted by the olive flesh of Amarinda. While waiting for my bed partner to wake I thought over what had happened the previous day. Despite the fact that Sister Murdock had said we were unable to leave, it was evident that I could phone up whomever I liked on the outside. Perhaps Katerina would have stopped me if I'd asked for the police, but she certainly couldn't have known that I wasn't going to cry for help from my mother, or Peter.

So although Athelstan Hall was physically a prison it wasn't really secure, in practical terms. I could have got out. I stayed because to invoke help would have felt cowardly and would have been an admission of failure. Perhaps Sister Murdock's strange methods actually *were* character building.

But why then was I still so determined to escape? If all it took was a phone call, why was I still seriously contemplating paying a visit to the gardener's utility room that afternoon? I knew what he would want from me. So my going there must mean I was willing to give it to him. Perhaps I really wanted to give it to him. Perhaps Sally had finally taken over Sarah's will, rather like Mr Hide dominating Dr Jekyll.

That morning, for the first time, I joined in with the other girls on Sister Murdock's set program. It was a savage business. She carried a short riding crop and was clearly more than willing to use it. We did plenty of physical exercise, including a run round the grounds, marshalled by Lance, Pearce and Spike, still wearing their masks but dressed in tracksuits.

Then Lance gave us a serious class on self-defence that I found genuinely valuable, though his ability to demonstrate the role of an attacker was severely hampered by his dragon's head. We even tackled some purely cerebral puzzles of logic, something I would normally have no time for, but which I actually got absorbed in when it was a team exercise.

But it all seemed a little half-hearted – a little forced. The main event, I soon realised, was the day's truth session, just before lunch. And even though I hadn't yet witnessed what was to happen I found myself having serious qualms. Being beaten with the riding crop or the paddle was downright painful, but that's all it was; the pain passed. Truth is forever. I remained extremely fearful about what would happen when I was put in the hot seat. I still had no idea what I might say, but I guessed it would be very difficult to say nothing at all, and that was indeed born out by the morning's encounter. However, despite my apprehension, I found myself becoming totally absorbed in the extraction of the truth, to the point, I must confess, of yielding to my curiosity and behaving quite rudely.

It was Millicent who was to be scrutinised. I still had a kindred feeling towards her because of our drinking competition on the first night. She looked very shy and self-effacing – partly because of the rather severe clothes she always wore. But there was plenty of energy in her eyes and that, together with the shyness, made me intrigued to know how she had arrived at Athelstan.

'I'll tell you what I know about Millicent,' said Sister Murdock, by way of introduction, 'and then she must take up the story.

'She was brought here last Sunday afternoon by her husband. He told me that he loves her very much indeed and he believes that she loves him too. However, in the three years they have been married he claims that she has had four affairs to his certain knowledge, and fears the number of her indiscretions may be even higher than that. He described himself as being at the end of his tether and gave me his blessing to do whatever I could to persuade Millicent to "settle down", as he put it. He said he didn't care what methods I used, or how severe they might be, either physically or mentally. The fact that she came here willingly convinces me that she too wants to resolve a situation that is intolerable to both her husband and herself.'

Millicent shuffled uneasily. She was the sort of person one wanted to see happy. From her looks she was also the last person one would expect to have had a string of affairs. Did men regularly chase her, or were the affairs of her own making?

Sister Murdock continued. 'Your husband also told me, Millicent, that you had been married before, for less than two years. Perhaps you could start by telling us about that.'

Millicent gave a surly shrug. 'I married too young, only just eighteen, to a dentist called Gary, who seemed to me the pillar of respectability,' she started. 'We'd been going out together for six or seven months before that. He was my first lover. He was ten years older than me, and he seemed to me to be wealthy and sophisticated. I thought he was fantastic.'

'So why did the marriage break up?' asked Elspeth, the brash redhead. 'Were you unfaithful to him, too?'

'No.' Millicent paused. 'I guess it simply didn't work out.'

Sister Murdock's crop flashed out and caught Millicent a stinging blow across the thigh, through her dress. She flinched and bit her lip, but did not cry out.

'That's no sort of an answer for a truth session,' Sister Murdock admonished. 'You know as well as we do that marriages do not fail simply because things don't work out. There is always a reason, sometimes many reasons. Are you being honest when you say you were faithful to him?'

'Yes, I promise,' Millicent insisted, rubbing her thigh ruefully. 'I... well, I looked up to him. Then I found out he wasn't quite as wonderful as I'd thought.'

'Go on.' Sister Murdock lowered the crop.

'What am I to tell you?' Millicent seemed to be searching for something suitable to say. 'He had... well, he had nasty habits in bed,' she said weakly.

'What are you saying?' I gasped, sensing what we were about to hear.

Millicent sighed with embarrassment. 'You know... he stuck it up my back passage,' she whispered, her cheeks flushing prettily. 'The very first time we made love, and every time thereafter.

'It sounds like a joke, now I'm telling you all about it,' she went on, looking a little more relaxed now her secret was out. 'But I was besotted by him, so how could I refuse him? What else could I do but do what I could to please him?'

And so the confession and the soul-searching went on, and it transpired that her loose behaviour was some misguided revenge on men for deception she'd suffered at the hands of Gary. Unfortunately, the only two who could suffer would be Millicent's husband, and Millicent. I have to say that I found the whole episode a little unconvincing, but I couldn't put my finger on why, and the occasional flicks of the crop dispensed by Sister Murdock seemed to lack just a little conviction.

Anyway, I put the strange feeling of doubt to the back of my mind and the session ended with various suggestions of how she could cure her wayward activities being put forward by me and some of the other girls.

For my part I was quite proud of my little piece of psychoanalysis, and of my proposed solution – I'll not go into the details – though I still didn't fancy being the one on the spot.

Thinking about the morning's activities, it seemed to me that everything would have been *reasonably* sane – aside from the men in their masks – if it weren't for Sister Murdock and her wretched crop. Thankfully she had left me alone, but unfortunately I had a nasty notion as to why this might be. I sensed I was being set up for a showdown at the evening meal, and the inevitable forfeit. But if I kow-towed to her and sneaked in early she would have won the battle of wills. If I stood my ground and arrived last I would have won the confrontation, but I now knew for certain what I could expect by way of a beating. I did not relish that, but I also knew my week at Athelstan would be pointless unless I courted, received, and triumphed over such punishment.

On the other hand, I could still try to escape. Okay, so I

could have rung Kendrick and told him to pick me up, but that would have been to admit defeat to Sister Murdock just as surely as if I'd gone down to dinner at five o'clock. Escaping under my own steam, on the other hand, would outwit her and therefore strike a victory to me. And it would avoid a beating. For both reasons, fellating a foul-smelling stranger did not seem such a terrible price to pay.

So that afternoon found me tapping on the door of the utility room once again. The man opened it and ushered me in possessively, and I noted a glint of excitement in the eyes that were partially visible through the holes in the mask.

'Are… are you going to keep your promise today?' I asked, feeling intimidated by his intensity.

'Yep,' he said, 'for five hundred and another suck.'

'But how do I know I can trust you?' I asked.

'Because I say so,' he said simply.

I knew I had no choice but to go along with his demands, but I was not so naïve as to suppose that I could trust him when his sexual energy was spent and when the time came for him to unlock the door – so I had a plan.

I dropped to my knees, unzipped his trousers and got to work. Strangely, the more abrupt and mercenary our arrangement the more exciting I found it.

I worked away with a will until the object of my attention was stiff and turgid. I have to admit that, although I saw myself in the role of a clever young woman about to outwit a churlish gardener, I found the presence of such a rampant staff in my mouth genuinely exciting. It was so aggressive, so bursting with life that once again I felt as if I had the very core of the man in my grasp. One moment I wanted to coax and cosset that core, and the next I had visions of snuffing his manhood out with one simple, well-timed bite.

I heard him begin to groan and knew he was coming to the boil, and so I abruptly pulled back.

'Don't stop now, bitch,' he hissed.

'I don't trust you,' I blurted. 'You'll get what you want from me and then you'll still leave me locked in.'

'No, I won't,' he insisted. 'Jesus, bitch, don't stop now!'

His rampant staff was rigid and swollen, too aroused to be assuaged except by fulfilment. I had timed things well.

'Unlock the door then,' I coaxed.

'No,' he said, 'you'll try to get away and leave me like this.'

'I won't, I promise,' I said. 'Besides, you're stronger than me, you could easily stop me.'

It was true enough, so he didn't pause for long. Swearing under his breath he fumbled in his trouser pocket, produced a key and unlocked the door.

'Okay, I've done it,' he grunted. 'Now finish the job.'

I prepared myself to accept the inevitable inundation, the taste of success, but he hung on longer than I expected, grittily prolonging his enjoyment and my subjugation. I was very tired by this time, but thankfully he once again grasped my head between his hands and pumped it back and forth, as if I was a cheap doll, and I just let it happen.

The flood nearly overwhelmed me, but I was determined to have my way. At the height of his climax I reached up for the lapels of his dreadful old gardening jacket and tugged it down around his arms, trapping them by his sides. Then, without pausing to check on the effectiveness of my assault, I jumped to my feet and made a desperate run for it.

# Chapter Twelve

I ran across the open area to the nearest bushes, feeling absolutely elated at my mini victory. I had outwitted the salacious gardener, and Sister Murdock to boot. It was a wonderful feeling. But whatever I did I mustn't get caught now. That would ruin everything, make a nonsense of my achievement, and no doubt call down some extra punishment.

Fortunately the garden was an ideal one for concealment, shrubs and trees everywhere, with a few lawns I could easily avoid. To tell the truth I had no idea rhododendrons could grow so thickly in England. It was like struggling through the undergrowth of a jungle. My strategy was just to get as far as I could from the house. Speed was essential. It seemed unlikely the gardener would raise the alarm and thus admit his involvement in my escape, but I couldn't be sure of that.

After about a hundred yards I encountered the perimeter wall, which I'd been able to see from my window. But it was high, certainly over ten feet. Even though there were fruit trees trained against it in many places it was still far too difficult for me to attempt to climb. What would I do when I got to the top? Jump?

So I turned right instead and set off round the boundary of the property, confident that I must eventually encounter the twin gates, even if I'd turned the wrong way and had to make a full circuit.

Becoming increasingly breathless I struggled on, snagging my slacks on the blackberries that grew wild in the uncultivated parts of the garden. The wall seemed to go on forever, and always built to the same formidable height. I began to grow apprehensive, remembering how imposing the gates had seemed upon arrival just a few days earlier, and reluctantly accepting for the first time that they would almost certainly be locked.

And I was right.

When I finally reached them they were closed and securely locked, and of equal height to the wall with spikes on top. I was done for!

Totally dispirited, I didn't even bother to go right up to them, but I certainly did curse myself for not foreseeing or planning for such an eventuality.

From my hiding-place in the undergrowth I could see closed-circuit cameras trained on the drive and on the road. No doubt the gates could be opened remotely if a car was seen approaching, as must have happened when Peter and I first arrived. I could remain in cover and wait for someone to arrive or leave and slip out before the gates closed again, but that was really clutching at straws.

I thought back on what it had cost me to get this far. Damn the gardener! He must have played along with the whole thing, knowing that my escape from the house itself was worthless. I turned back and started retracing my steps along the base of the wall. I'd previously decided it would be too dangerous to try climbing one of the many trees – not having much of a head for heights – but now I was utterly determined not to be beaten, no matter the risk.

A beautiful old elm leaned tantalisingly towards the wall. I clambered up the sloping trunk with no difficulty. It was so easy I felt encouraged to go on. But what would I do to get down the other side of the wall?

In the event I never put that question to the test. I was edging out towards the top of the wall along one of the side branches, and I still had about a metre to go when I heard an ominous crack. I froze, and then looked cautiously back. The branch I was on was rotten! The only thing that had stopped it breaking was that its far end had come to rest on the wall itself.

I was now seriously unhappy with my situation. I was balanced precariously ten feet up with an extremely prickly bed of brambles directly beneath me. Should I go on and rely on the wall carrying my weight?

No, I chickened out.

I had to go back. I began to shuffle back along the branch in very undignified retreat, resolutely avoiding looking down. Then, without the slightest warning, the branch gave up the struggle and I found myself plunging straight down.

Luckily I'd managed to move back far enough to miss the brambles, but with a loud grunt I landed in the long grass, the bone-crunching impact knocking the wind from my lungs.

Cursing myself again for being so hopeless, I opened my eyes as the pain eased slightly, and saw someone standing over me. Staring impassively down at me, the gardener offered no assistance, so I gingerly got to my feet.

'I'll... I'll go back to the house,' I said lamely. 'I've been very silly.'

And 'silly' was an understatement. For thereon in I had to simply admit defeat and put the best face on it that I could manage. So I set off up the drive towards the house, pretending to admire the flowers as if out for an afternoon stroll, knowing someone might be watching me. As I approached the front door I deliberately went over to one of the flowerbeds and sniffed some roses.

And sure enough, Sister Murdock soon appeared at the front door, so I pre-empted her.

'What a simply delightful garden, Sister Murdock,' I said, as brightly as my dampened spirits would allow.

'We're very proud of it,' she acknowledged, 'though you'll appreciate we don't normally allow guests to wander unaccompanied.'

'Oh, you should,' I said. 'You're far too security conscious. At a mind-broadening establishment like this you should allow your guests to make the deliberate decision as to whether they want to stay or leave.'

And then, knowing I'd gone as far as was sensible and that my 'advice' would only infuriate her, I hastily changed the subject.

'Sister Murdock,' I said, 'could I have a word with you in your office, please?'

'You may,' she said stiffly, and ushered me inside the house and into her office.

'I've had what I hope may be an interesting idea,' I explained, once she had closed the door and sat at her desk, leaving me standing. 'I'm assuming you're in the business of running Athelstan Hall because you want to make money.'

'An endeavour that doesn't make a profit soon ceases to exist,' she replied warily.

'And I assume that you're not too finicky about how you do that, provided you stay within the bounds of the law,' I went on. 'You've already demonstrated that your techniques are very far removed from those of the conventional encounter group, or even a psychiatric institution.'

She nodded, so I proceeded to tell her Amarinda's story in full, culminating in the dilemma that now faced her. Should she marry a rich, considerate man who loved her but who would not permit her to stray one inch from the path of total propriety? Or should she use her body to earn good money, whilst losing the respect, support and friendship of her family and her community in doing so?

'And how do you propose we should help her?' Sister Murdock asked, genuinely interested.

'Well, it occurred to me that there may be hundreds, if not thousands, of women caught essentially between the same two stools. Ninety-nine percent of them will choose the path of conventionality, and that's exactly how things should be. But they will still spend the rest of their days a prey to the knowledge that they have missed out on some facet of life that could have offered a very special thrill or fulfilment.

'And, at a suitable price, you could provide that thrill, that fulfilment.'

She studied me for a while, and then asked, 'And how do I do that?'

'Well,' I went on, 'in Amarinda's case it's obvious. A couple of times a year she asks her rich husband whether she can come down to Athelstan Hall for a week, to meet earlier friends, or to lose some weight, or to shake her out of a depression, she could say. He wouldn't refuse. Then while she's here she could go on a clandestine trip to Soho to strut on the stage and earn the temporary adulation she craves. You could accompany her, together with Lance or

Pearce to ensure she doesn't get into trouble. She'd pay well for that excitement, I'm sure, and her husband and family would have no idea such an adventure had ever occurred.'

Sister Murdock stared at me, thinking my suggestion over.

'It seems to me that Amarinda's source of excitement is an unusual one, to say the least,' she said at last.

'Unusual only because it's socially unacceptable,' I pointed out. 'But anyway, I didn't mean your activities should be confined to satisfying Amarinda. A discreet encounter group could provide any number of services for a lady who was able to pay; anything one would be too ashamed to do at home. Sex with another woman, for example. It may leave some cold, but at least they could try it to assuage that nagging uncertainty.'

Sister Murdock leaned forward on her elbows. 'Are you suggesting we should cater for men, too?'

'No. If you did that you'd be called a brothel. Anyway, I have the feeling men are already well looked after. There are lots of discreet clubs in London. Men have the nerve to go to such establishments. With women it's much more difficult. That's why they need somewhere as a cover. And what better place than Athelstan Hall?'

Sister Murdock thought for a few minutes, then she said, 'I'm interested. What exactly should I do about it?'

'Make Amarinda a test case,' I proposed. 'Tomorrow night, drive up to London and put her on the stage at *The Good Ship Venus*. In front of a full audience. The proprietor's not going to complain, is he?'

Sister Murdock stared at me for a couple more minutes, and then made a decision. 'All right, I'll do it,' she said.

'But there's one proviso.'

'And what would that be?' I asked warily.

'It's your idea,' she said, smirking, 'so you can come with us and go up on the stage, too.'

I gasped. In truth it was what I had dreamed of while Amarinda was relating her story to me. But it would be insane.

'Impossible!' I exclaimed. 'I'd be recognised.'

Wrong answer. I should simply have refused, point-blank.

'Not necessarily,' she said slyly. 'We could hire the skills of a make-up expert. You could be unidentifiable.'

'No, no,' I refused, shaking my head. 'It's quite out of the question.'

Sister Murdock stared quizzically at me as if to suggest that I was perhaps protesting a little too hard. And in a sense, she was right. Amarinda's story had stirred me. What would it feel like, I wondered, to stand up on a stage, a couple of feet from a dozen sweaty faces, all staring at me? This could be my one chance in a lifetime to find out. But no, no, it was quite mad!

'I'll try what you suggest,' Sister Murdock repeated doggedly, 'but only on that one condition. You have to take part, too.'

Suddenly I burst into tears. 'Why are you so cruel to me?' I demanded.

'I have to be cruel to be kind,' she replied, smugly.

Stuff that, I thought, she was just kinky. But, somewhat uneasily, I realised she might have a point. Earlier I had, under the influence of Athelstan's madhouse, and by self-analysis, decided what I had to do when I got back with Peter. I'd got to let myself go, and stop being frightened of the fact that sex made me lose my self-control. But what had changed? I'd known all along that by hook or by crook I'd got to persuade him to take me. What if I begged him to come to bed the moment I got home? Might I not still fight him off at the last minute, inhibited by the same stupid fear that had made my short life with him a misery? Sister Murdock was right; I had already submitted myself to some quite outrageous acts while I'd been at Athelstan Hall. Why not one more, just to show that I could take the worst the world could throw at me?

'All right,' I said, abruptly.

She smiled disconcertingly, and said, 'Very well, I'll make the arrangements.'

The afternoon's truth session was Elspeth's, and she was rumoured to have a drink problem. She was a very striking looker, certainly the most immediately photogenic of us all; tall, statuesque, with a mane of red hair. Sister Murdock stood her unmercifully in the middle of the room, with the rest of us seated around her in a circle.

'Stand up straight,' Sister Murdock commanded, 'and face away from me.'

For a moment I saw Elspeth show some resistance, but then she shrugged and did as she was told. Might as well accept it and get the session over with, she seemed to be thinking. Sister Murdock lazily lashed out at her rump with her riding crop like a cricketer trying to get his length right, Elspeth's sharp intake of breath no doubt convincing her that her eye was in and that a long innings could be expected. 'Good,' she said. 'Everything is in order. Elspeth, your husband brought you here, did he not, with the entreaty that I should do whatever was in my power to stop your excessive drinking.'

Elspeth shrugged and said nothing, her long red hair tossed back over her shoulders. Her proud figure was nothing less than spectacular, and she held herself like the trained model she was.

'Do you agree you have a drink problem?' Sister Murdock asked bluntly.

'No, not at all,' she denied. 'I simply like the odd one or two.'

'Your husband, Morgan, said you get through on average a bottle of gin every day, and that takes some serious practice. Tell me again you have no problem.'

'I don't think of it as a problem' Elspeth giggled. 'I drink, I get drunk, I fall down. I'm very good at it. Where's the problem?'

The riding crop flailed angrily. 'Don't be facetious!' Sister Murdock bellowed.

Elspeth rubbed herself gingerly. 'Sorry,' she said. 'It was just a joke.'

'This is no joke,' Sister Murdock said firmly. 'You have to cut down. Morgan said he'd send you here for a week every month until you'd learned your lesson. Do you want that?'

'Um, no,' Elspeth said, becoming more serious.

'So tell me you'll reform.'

'Why do you let Elspeth drink at mealtimes?' I asked Sister Murdock, trying to turn the attack against her.

'That's surely obvious,' she replied. 'I want her to cut down through her own choice. While she's here she can drink as much as she pleases, though her buttocks will suffer for it.'

It still did not make sense. One achieved one's aim,

surely, either by coercion or by persuasion. Sister Murdock did not seem to have decided which, and her approach was predicated, I was sure, by a desire to exercise her whip as often and as painfully as possible.

'But why don't we ask her *why* she drinks?' I insisted.

The truth was that I was a little frightened of becoming like Elspeth. To be sure, I had refrained from excessive alcohol since my lapse at Lindos, but now I was married to Peter the temptation was painfully obvious; I didn't have enough to do during the day, and the drinks cabinet was overflowing with possible distractions.

With heavy sarcasm Sister Murdock handed me the riding crop. 'Go on, then,' she challenged. 'You ask her.'

'Well?' I said, a little awkwardly. 'Elspeth, when did you start drinking heavily?'

'At about the same time I got married, I suppose,' Elspeth replied. 'Two years ago.'

'Why?' I quizzed. 'Isn't it a happy marriage?'

'Oh goodness me, that's not the problem!' she snorted indignantly. 'I love Morgan with all my heart. That's why I'm standing here, taking this crap. I promised him I'd come here without a fuss, and by hook or by crook I'm going to get through this week.'

'And when you get home, will you cut down?' I went on.

Elspeth thought quite hard. 'That's a tricky one,' she admitted. 'If I *do* cut back noticeably Morgan will see this crackpot cure as having been to some degree successful. So when I lapse back to my former ways he'll think it's worth forking out another grand for a top-up week. Instead, it might be better in the long run to go back to him as drunk as a newt. Then he'll just give up.'

Temporarily overcome by the heady intoxication of holding a riding whip I lashed out at poor Elspeth. 'Don't be facetious,' I said, inadvertently mimicking Sister Murdock.

The others laughed, but the dark look on Sister Murdock's face warned me that I might be storing up future misery for myself.

'Did you have a job before you were married?' I asked.

Elspeth gave me a sideways look, and nodded.

'What was it?' As I said the words I sensed I might be stepping into murky waters.

'I was a model,' she told us. 'A glamour model. And I was quite successful.' There was a touch of resentment in her voice, and suddenly I twigged.

'Oh my goodness,' I gasped. 'You're Elspeth Ellis.' I simply hadn't recognised her.

'Fame doesn't last long, does it?' she said, looking disgruntled.

'No, no, it was my fault,' I hastened.

But the damage was already done; I had pinpointed the alcohol-induced deterioration of her looks, and I'd also drawn attention to the fact that in the couple of years or so since she'd dropped out of the public view she had already become forgettable. Feeling embarrassed, I rushed on blindly.

'So is that the problem?' I babbled. 'Your husband wouldn't let you pose naked any more, since your marriage?'

'He wouldn't have stopped me,' she sulked. 'But it's a bloodthirsty profession, and I was ready enough to pull out.'

'You say that,' I said, 'but perhaps you miss the publicity, the eager looks from other men.'

'Perhaps,' she conceded. 'But it's irrelevant. I'm too old to start again now.'

'Hardly,' I argued. 'Stop drinking, do a little fitness work, and you could easily be right back in there with the best. Are you sure you're telling the truth when you say Morgan wouldn't object?'

'You're on the wrong track,' she said. 'I'm too old. Sixteen is when you start, nineteen or twenty when you finish.'

I could remember several famous names who had lasted a lot longer than that. 'I don't agree,' I said firmly. 'Go on, take your dress off. Let us judge.'

She shook her head. I caught some looks from a couple of the girls. I seemed to be saying something wrong again, though I'd merely wanted to pay her a compliment.

'Well, why not?' Sister Murdock put in. 'You've surely a body to be proud of. Let us all see it.'

My own request had seemed sincere but naïve, but in contrast Sister Murdock's seemed malicious. Still, I could tell from one or two interested faces that she and I weren't the only ones to want a first-hand peek at such a famous body.

'Well, all right, bugger you all,' said Elspeth sourly.

She began to undress and I found that my expectations – that she was already losing her figure – were far from the truth. As she stood before us in her underwear one could only feel an extraordinary envy. Her skin was clear and unblemished, her bosom firm and proud, her waist narrow. But then an odd thing occurred; she took off her panties before she removed her bra. I suppose there are no written rules on this sort of thing, but it looked strangely unnatural to see a woman bottomless, but not topless.

'What do you think of it so far?' she enquired, but it came out as a scowl, not a joke.

'Lovely,' I replied, speaking honestly.

Then she removed her bra and there was an instant chorus of gasps; her breasts were still magnificent, but her right one had a savage scar right across it.

'Oh Elspeth, I'm so sorry,' I tried weakly. 'I had no idea…' A feeble response, but what was there to say? No wonder she'd fallen into drink.

'So you see why I stopped modelling,' she said bitterly. 'You can't do glamour photos without showing your breasts, can you? And you can't be photographed in close-up showing such a monstrosity.'

There was an uneasy silence, which I sought to break. 'Is it public knowledge?' I asked.

'Oh no,' she said, shaking her head, 'and I'm trusting you all to keep it a secret. Imagine what a field day the Sunday papers would have.' She paused. 'And as for finding a cure for my drinking, you can see it may be a little difficult.'

'Nevertheless, you must,' I insisted. 'If you go on at your present rate you'll be dead by the time you're thirty, and painfully ugly by about this time next year.'

'Thanks,' she said ruefully.

'I'm sorry, Elspeth,' I went on, 'but you have to tell us how it happened. This is a truth session, and I'd rather you told us willingly than waited for Sister Murdock or me to beat it out of you.'

Elspeth shrugged. 'I'd rather not,' she said. 'There's nothing edifying about the story at all. And what makes it worse is that it was entirely my own fault.'

'So you feel guilty?' Sister Murdock said. 'Well, let us be the judges of that.'

'Huh!' she snorted. 'There's nothing to debate.'

'But go on anyway,' I urged.

She glanced angrily at me, and then at Sister Murdock. There was nowhere to hide.

'Oh, all right,' she complied, reluctantly. 'What a complete misery this place is!

'It happened one night when I was out with Morgan, before we were married. As I said, I love Morgan, and I think I always have, ever since I met him. He's kind, thoughtful, and humorous. But he's also terribly square – almost a party-pooper. It used to make me very irritable.'

'Were you at a party?' I asked.

'Yes,' she confirmed. 'It was Carla's twenty-first. She was my best friend. She's a model too, and it was that sort of a do – all very flamboyant and arty, photographers and agents, most of them gay. Morgan stuck out like a sore thumb. I was so embarrassed for him. But of course he didn't even notice how different he was.'

She paused and glanced around uncomfortably. I could see she was desperate for a drink, but no one offered her one.

'The party was in a marquee,' she continued, 'on Carla's parents' lawn, and it was just about over. It was certainly well after two o'clock in the morning and Morgan was desperate to go home, but I hung on, just to spite him. Then these three bikers appeared – gatecrashers, obviously – who had been drawn by the music. They sported all the obligatory badges of their group, long hair, beards, worn jeans, waistcoats and earrings. We should have called the police and had them thrown out, but I was in a show-off mood. Morgan and I were dancing cheek-to-cheek in the middle of the marquee. I knew the bikers were eyeing me up, but drunk as I was, I liked it.

'Morgan whispered in my ear that we should go into the house – everyone else had – but I carried on dancing. I wanted the bikers to want me. I moved lasciviously against Morgan, allowing my short skirt to ride up.

'Then I pulled his reluctant hands down onto my bottom. He was appalled. "There's going to be trouble," he muttered in my ear.

'Soon the bikers left their corner and began to move in time with the slow music, coming closer and closer till they surrounded us; it seemed they felt none of the normal constraints of accepted behaviour. They moved in till they were pressing against me – till I was the filling in a sandwich of four men. Morgan tried to pull free but I still held him tight. Meanwhile three alien pairs of hands were on me, exploring my body, tugging at my clothing.

'He tried to drag me away but I was having none of it. I remember whispering, "Don't be a silly, Morgan, it'll be fun." The grim future tense in that remark made it plain at last just how far I intended to go. I could see the horror on his face. Should he manhandle me to the house? Run inside for help? Call the police, even? In the end he did nothing, lost and bewildered, out of his depth, afraid that for the first time he was seeing the real me.

'The bikers bore me down to the grass and stripped me, and I let them quite willingly, responding to their avaricious kisses. The first one had his way with me, and by that time Morgan had left the tent. I think he was crying. The second one did it too, and I was still longing for more. They poured whisky over my body and licked it off, and I encouraged them. Can you believe that? But by now they were seriously drunk, and the third one was an animal. He fell on me, squeezing, pinching, pulling. I began to scream with pain but that was the wrong thing to do. That was what he wanted, what he enjoyed.'

She stopped. We all sat there, aghast. I couldn't stand the silence. 'So what happened?' I gasped. 'Did Morgan come back? Was there a fight?'

'No, no fight,' she said quietly. 'The first two bikers were standing there laughing. The third was far too strong for me. The bastard took me and then he simply slashed my breast with a knife. For fun. Then they made a run for it – off on their bikes.'

I burst into tears from sheer shock, leapt to my feet and threw my arms around her. 'Oh Elly,' I said, 'how could they do such a thing? Couldn't the police catch them?'

'Not much point, really,' she said. 'The damage had been done, and catching them would have made the whole sorry story public knowledge. And, as I said, no one was more to blame for what happened than me. So don't you think I've a perfect right to drink myself silly?'

She was right, of course, though I knew we must not admit it. 'No, no,' I tried. 'Morgan still married you, even after that. You owe it to him to keep your looks.'

'Yes, at least some good came out of the fiasco,' she admitted. 'I realised at last what a real saint he is. I'd known all along, of course, but it really brought it home to me. Also, I learned humility overnight. I was a real bitch before that. Now I'm almost human, and I wish I could stop drinking for Morgan's sake.'

'And you can,' I encouraged. 'Look, Elspeth, I can't begin to appreciate what you went through, so I've no right to preach. But I do know that plenty of other people in the public gaze suffer horrendous traumas and still manage to survive.'

'So, tell me what they do?' she challenged.

'Well…' I really didn't have a clue. 'You could appear on talk shows,' I fished, without much conviction. 'You could become a pop star… you could write your memoirs.'

Elspeth pondered for a while, and then shook her head. 'I've no talent, is surely the answer to that. All I've ever done is pose for photographs. I have nothing interesting to say, I can't sing, and I wouldn't have a clue how to write a book.'

I thought hard. 'Okay,' I said at length, 'since I'm holding the whip it seems I'm in charge, and this is what I'm prescribing for your problem. You can continue to drink as much as you like – right? But you do need to do something that'll give you your self-respect back, something that's in the public eye that you can make a success of. And I bet I know what that something is.'

'Really?' she said, somewhat sarcastically. 'Tell me.'

'You must start a modelling agency,' I said excitedly, suddenly realising I might be on to something. 'You've already got the name. Girls will fall over themselves to be one of your protégées. Yes…' I could see it all now, 'as soon as I get out of here I'm going to tell Peter to loan you the capital to get started. And you're going to feel guilty as hell if you don't pay it back. You're going to work so hard on making it a success that you won't have time to get drunk.'

'Come on, it's hopeless,' she said negatively.

I suddenly became angry, and handed the riding crop back to Sister Murdock. 'Hit her with that,' I said. Sister

Murdock raised her eyebrows, but lashed out anyway. Elspeth shied away, staring at me as if I'd betrayed her.

'Elspeth,' I said patiently, 'do you want to come back here every couple of months for continued abuse?'

She yelped as the crop landed again, and shook her head.

'Then resign yourself to the effort of having to start afresh, to build your life again from scratch. That's what you're shying away from.'

She looked at me, clearly unsettled by the passion in my voice.

'Elspeth,' I continued, 'I'll bet you had to submit to some pretty degrading treatment, while you were fighting to become a known model.'

'And some,' she said bitterly.

'But you could make it right for the girls you employ,' I pointed out, trying a different tack. 'Run a clean business. Don't publish anything tacky. Am I getting through to you?'

She glared at me, sullenly.

'I'm ashamed to say I've never suffered at all,' I said quietly. 'I hate to admit this in front of Sister Murdock, but coming to this place has made me realise what a self-centred bitch I've been. I've never done a thing to deserve my good fortune, I've simply been blessed with a pretty face. And your misfortune has made me realise just how unjustifiably lucky I've been. Let me pay you back by getting you going again.'

She stared at me for a long time. Then she drew herself up to her full height and pulled her shoulders back.

'You're right,' she said quietly, a sparkle returning to her eyes. 'I'll do it. I really will.'

# Chapter Thirteen

What do you wear when you know you're going to be spanked? None of the fashion magazines I've read have ever addressed that vital question. I opted for a short blouse that stopped just above my navel, and tight trousers that flattered my buttocks.

'I want to look my best for the occasion,' I muttered to the mirror.

This bravado was not as daft as it might seem. I was to be stretched over a table and beaten by a nun whose moral character and general sanity were both seriously questionable. I could cringe abjectly from the pain that was to come, or I could confront it by deliberately exaggerating the spanking's sexual content. With the short blouse top I knew that when I leaned forward the undersides of my breasts would be visible from behind, and hoped their beauty would be like a slap in the face to a dried-up old hag like Sister Murdock.

At about a quarter past five I made my way downstairs with some trepidation but no lessening of pride or resolve. I deliberately passed the door of the dining hall but did not go in. Instead I walked along to the secretary's office.

'I'm expecting Peter to phone me at the same time he did last night,' I explained to Katerina. 'Can I come in?'

'Of course, Lady Sarah,' she said, and then there was a silence she eventually felt obliged to break. 'How are you enjoying your stay with us?' she asked conversationally.

'Well, "enjoying" is perhaps too strong a word. It's an interesting course; stimulating, I would say, rather than enjoyable.'

'Most of our young ladies regard it as time well spent,' she claimed. 'Discomfort is simply relative, I've found. I often wish I could join in with some of the more strenuous activities instead of being tied down in this office.'

I pricked up my ears. What was she trying to tell me? That she would welcome some of the abuse we had all been taking? While I was searching for a probing but camouflaged question the phone rang. It was Peter.

'How's it going?' he asked.

'Oh, not too bad,' I said non-committally. 'I'm getting used to Sister Murdock's stranger habits. I even had a civilised conversation with her this afternoon. How about you?'

'It's hectic, but no more than I expected,' he said. 'I'll tell you about it when I get home.'

Suddenly a vision of me stretched over the table and the stinging agony of the paddle returned. I could not take it. 'Peter, I…' I whispered.

'What, Sarah?' he asked. 'What were you going to say?'

I knew very well what I wanted to say, but nothing came out. This was a battle I had to win on my own. 'Nothing… I…' I faltered, 'well, I just wish you were home.'

'Soon, Sarah,' he promised. 'Maybe I'll be with you sooner than you think. Love you.'

His voice had seemed strangely emotional, full of longing. Why was I clowning around with a bunch of misfits when I had the perfect husband to love? I'd had enough of self-analysis. I already knew what I had to do to make Peter mine; love him unreservedly and let my feelings show.

I jerked back to the present. Katerina was staring at me.

'Are you all right, Lady Sarah?' she asked.

I nodded.

'It must be wonderful to be in love with such a fine man as Sir Peter,' she said sincerely. 'And to be loved in return.'

'Yes, it is,' I said absent-mindedly, still thinking of my impending doom. 'What's the time?'

'Just after six.'

'I'd better go into dinner.'

'I wish I could be in your place,' she said.

I had already shut the office door behind me before it dawned on me that her last remark might not simply refer to my life with Peter. Could she have meant she was willing to take my place in the dining hall?

I entered the hall and took my usual seat – the last one available. My trepidation dulled my appetite, but at least I could take some wine to ease my nerves. Hopefully it would deaden the pain to some extent. The minutes rushed by towards seven-thirty, which was when Sister Murdock made her speech. On the dot she appeared at the head of the table while the men distributed themselves around the room.

'Good evening, ladies,' she began. 'Today has been an eventful one. You may be glad to hear that Lady Sarah has suggested a remarkably simple solution to poor Amarinda's disagreement with her parents. We are going to give that a try tomorrow night, and it will hopefully mean that Amarinda will accept the hand of her parents' choice in marriage.

'Lady Sarah also featured in a serious lapse of security this afternoon when she wandered around the gardens unsupervised, and without any explanation as to how she got out of the house. I cannot, of course, allow such disobedience to go unmarked, and I shall have to add one more stroke to the beating she must receive for once again being last to dinner.' She looked at me severely, before adding, 'Lady Sarah, will you take your place willingly over the table, or must I ask Lance and Pearce to assist again?'

I got shakily to my feet. 'No,' I said, 'I can manage on my own, thank you. I prefer to deny them the pleasure of manhandling me.'

Pompous words, spoken to try and boost my own resolve. But, faced with the imminent punishment to come, I had in reality reverted to schoolgirl again, terrified of being humiliated in front of the other girls. The trouble was, as I made to lower my trousers, I was overcome by a violent need to dash to the ladies' to relieve myself of the evening's wine intake. I hesitated, and then asked, 'Sister Murdock, do I have your permission to go to the toilet?'

She shook her head with a malicious glint in her eye.

'Please,' I whimpered, 'this is urgent.' But she was unmoved. I cursed her under my breath. I watched as Spike walked over to the mantelpiece, took down the paddle and handed it to her. Then I bit my lip, dropped my trousers and panties and leaned forward over the table.

The first blow fell with astonishing swiftness before I was fully prepared, and against my will I let out a pitiful howl.

'That's all right, my dear,' gloated Sister Murdock, 'we have no objection to you expressing your feelings. You may well find it helps you come to terms with your punishment. We also recommend that you thank the administrator of your beating and ask her to deliver the next blow.'

I wanted to swear at the sadistic hag, but it would have achieved nothing other than make me look cheap. So instead I whispered hoarsely, 'Thank you, Sister Murdock. I'm ready for the next blow.'

As the vile implement of torture slapped against my defenceless flesh I clutched the table in desperate agony, and couldn't prevent myself from groaning in unison with the strike.

'Sister Murdock,' I simpered through clenched teeth. 'I won't be able to hold it.'

It sounded plaintive and pathetic; the last impression I wanted to give. Sister Murdock's response was typically cruel. She lashed out immediately and with all her remaining strength, and my world was once again filled with agony. I felt myself lose control. Hot fluid trickled down my legs to the floor. I sobbed in misery. How could I, Lady Sarah, have allowed myself to be so degraded?

The beating was over, so I forced myself stiffly upright, clawed desperately for my clothes, and ran.

# Chapter Fourteen

The following morning I was on my way down to breakfast when I heard a noise from another of the bedrooms. It sounded like a cry for help, so I pushed open the door and found Angie, the diminutive brunette, in bed on her front.

I asked her what was wrong.

'I'm tied down,' she complained, real concern in her eyes.

I went over and pulled the bedclothes away. Sure enough, she was spread-eagled with her wrists and ankles securely tied to the four corners of the bed, and to my surprise she was dressed as a schoolgirl; gymslip, shirt and tie, white ankle socks, the lot. Her hair had even been tied in a ponytail. It was most bizarre. I started to scrabble with the soft rope.

'Who did this?' I asked as I tried to free her.

'I don't know,' she said plaintively. 'When I woke up I couldn't move.'

'Did you put these clothes on?' I asked.

She shook her head.

'Then you must know who did,' I reasoned. 'It surely couldn't have been done without you realising.'

'I had too much wine last night,' she admitted shamefully. 'I don't remember a thing.'

I gave up on the knots in frustration. 'It's no good,' I cursed, 'I can't get them undone. I'll have to go down to the kitchen for a knife or something.'

I turned, only to find Sister Murdock in the doorway, smiling enigmatically.

'Is this your doing?' I asked.

'Of course it is,' she admitted without qualms, amusement in her eyes. 'Today is Angie's truth session. Yesterday she told me categorically she would not take part, so I've merely taken what measures were necessary to ensure her compliance.'

'But, you can't tie your guests down,' I complained. 'She paid to come here, and I think you'll find it's illegal.'

'She didn't pay, her husband did,' was Sister Murdock's matter-of-fact reply. 'Now leave her to ponder her predicament and come down to breakfast. I'll not hear another word on the matter.'

Thus defeated, I followed her down to the dining room.

When we'd finished eating Sister Murdock clapped her hands. 'Angie's truth session is scheduled for today,' she announced. 'She has shown a reluctance to co-operate, which I find quite unacceptable. So we shall be starting today's activities in her room. Will you all please follow me?'

We dutifully tripped up to Angie's room.

Once there Sister Murdock threw her bedclothes aside. Then she flipped up the back of her pleated gymslip and pulled her white knickers down just a little, so that her buttocks were exposed, pink and vulnerable. I stared at her squirming figure and reflected that she had the misfortune to look like the perfect victim. She was tiny, with a soft voluptuous body that seemed to cry out to be violated. Dressed as a schoolgirl, and with her buttocks peeping out from between her raised skirt and lowered knickers, the temptation to spank her was almost overwhelming. I silently scolded myself for harbouring such lurid thoughts.

'Angie is a very lucky young lady,' Sister Murdock said solemnly. 'She is married to a very wealthy French businessman, the director of a large communications conglomerate. He told me he dotes on her and would give her anything she wants. Yet he has deposited her here for a week, with the understanding that her stay will not be an easy one. Why do you think that is, Angie?'

'I... I don't know,' she stammered meekly.

At this point I half expected to hear the swish of the riding crop, but it was nowhere to be seen. Instead, Sister Murdock turned to Freya and said, 'Please give her a good hard smack.'

Freya's eyes gleamed and without question she lashed out at Angie's buttocks. Angie squealed and her back arched.

'I think you do know,' continued Sister Murdock.

'It... it'll be something to do with sex,' Angie muttered resentfully.

'Quite right.' Sister Murdock nodded. 'But then, wherever relationship problems exist you can be pretty sure that sex is the culprit, in some way or other.

'Jacques adores your body, Angie,' she went on. 'That is why he married you. His complaint is simply that you don't let him enjoy it in all the ways he would wish. Bluntly put, he says you are frigid.'

'Rubbish!' the poor girl squealed indignantly. 'He's a monster, that's the truth! If he had his way we'd be at it three or four times a night.'

I noticed the look on the faces of one or two of the other girls. I suspected we all thought, but no one said, that many a young lady of Angie's age would be grateful to change places with her, if the price or the prize was a man who wanted it three or four times a night.

'Jacques voiced his disappointment quite specifically,' Sister Murdock explained patiently. 'He did not actually complain that you would not allow him to make love as often as he would like. Instead he complained that you would not co-operate with a mild predilection he enjoys. Perhaps you will tell us what that predilection is.'

There was no reply, so Sister Murdock nodded to Millicent. 'It's your turn,' she said.

Millicent raised her eyebrows, and for a moment I thought she was about to object. But then she too slapped Angie's bottom as hard as she could. Angie winced and started crying.

'There really is no point in resisting,' Sister Murdock went on. 'I know the story because Jacques told me. So you might as well admit it to the others.' She paused, waiting for Angie to reply. But the girl merely lay there, so she nodded to Astrud who let swing eagerly, her hand lingering on the rapidly reddening globes.

To my surprise, despite crying from pain and anger, Angie still did not answer.

'This is your last chance,' Sister Murdock warned as she nodded to Elspeth, who struck quite uncompromisingly. On one level I was surprised that the girls, who should have been allies, were mistreating one of their number with such evident relish. But I sensed that they felt the way I did; Angie made such an irresistible target for spanking that none of them could resist the opportunity.

But still she lay there, sullen and silent.

'Very well,' said Sister Murdock, still unruffled, 'if that's the way you want it.' She picked up the internal phone on the bedside table and dialled one number. 'Katerina, be so good as to bring my riding crop up to Angie's room,' she ordered curtly.

We all waited in awe. This had suddenly become very serious. So far I had not seen Sister Murdock use her crop on any of the girls except through their clothing. If she beat Angie's unprotected buttocks she would surely mark her delicate flesh. I was sure her husband would not want that. Had Sister Murdock finally lost control of her own savage nature?

But when Katerina appeared with the riding crop an extraordinary thing happened. Sister Murdock took it from her and then said, 'Would you lean forward against that wall and raise your skirt, please?'

'Who, me?' said Katerina, clearly startled.

'Yes, you,' Sister Murdock confirmed. 'I should explain that Angie is refusing to describe to us an inclination her husband enjoys, despite receiving quite a severe spanking. So you are to act as her surrogate until she sees sense and gives in.'

The hair prickled on the back of my neck. This was incredible. But such was Sister Murdock's dominance that Katerina simply bit her lip and turned to lean against the nearest wall, lifting her skirt and offering her neat panty-clad bottom as an easy target. From her meek acquiescence I realised this wasn't the first time she had suffered in such a way. I recalled her ambiguous remarks from the previous evening, and it looked as though she was going to have her wish granted sooner rather than later.

Angie twisted her head round to look at her, aghast.

The crop swept the air and Katerina cried out in pain, her knees buckling from the shock.

'Hold your position,' snarled Sister Murdock, 'or it will be the worse for you!'

Gingerly, Katerina resumed her stance.

'This is unfair!' cried Angie. 'It's blackmail!'

'Of course it is,' replied Sister Murdock, 'and it will continue until you succumb.'

She lashed out again, but this time Katerina seemed to have found some inner strength and she took the blow stoically, with barely a sound.

It dawned on me that if she had been beaten before and if she still stayed in Sister Murdock's employ it was because she expected or even welcomed such punishment. But Angie was crying, and I could not imagine how she must feel, being the direct cause of the innocent secretary's treatment.

'All right, all right, I'll tell you!' she wailed, defeated despite not feeling the bite of the crop on her own flesh. 'He... he wants me to dress up,' she confessed quietly.

'And is that so dreadful?' asked the spiteful witch.

To me the revelation certainly seemed to be something of an anti-climax. 'What does he want you to dress up as?' I asked, a little stupidly, as it turned out.

Angie hesitated again, and that was all the excuse Sister Murdock needed to weigh into Katerina one more time.

'Isn't it obvious?' whimpered Angie, her token resistance broken. 'Mainly he wants me to dress up as a schoolgirl.'

I should obviously have guessed. Feeling a little silly I said, 'But you're dressed as a schoolgirl now – is it so bad? Surely it's only a bit of fun?'

'Is it?' Angie snorted. 'None of you want to make love to me while I am dressed like this.'

Well, that was open to debate.

'Tell me,' I went on hurriedly, hoping none of the others had noticed the colour the enticing prospect had brought to my cheeks, 'has he ever asked you to dress up as anything else; a French maid, for instance?'

Angie nodded miserably. 'Sometimes he wants me to wear a silky maid's outfit, and sometimes a nurse's uniform with a low top that reveals my cleavage, and a ridiculously short skirt that shows my suspenders and panties every time I sit or bend over.'

'So that's why you wanted to avoid your truth session,' I said thoughtfully.

'What... what do you mean?' she asked cautiously.

'Well, you think Jacques finds your sexy clothing more of a turn on than you, and that naturally knocks your confidence and self-esteem. You think that without the allure of the outfits he won't want you.'

Angie remained pensive for a few minutes, and then nodded grudgingly. 'But I don't see why I should have to pander to him. Surely I'm attractive enough for him as I am. Do you think I'm an attractive and sexy girl?'

There was a restrained murmur and nodding from those standing over the invitingly nubile girl – but not from Sister Murdock or Katerina, of course.

'So if Jacques isn't a bit weird why does he want me to dress up whenever we have sex?' she went on. 'And why does he want it so much he's willing to pay money to have me brought to this awful place?'

'I believe,' I said, 'that your husband's little fantasies are nothing like as worrying as you make out. A lot of men love such titillation, and it's all pretty harmless.'

Angie thought for a long time. 'You… you might be right,' she eventually conceded quietly.

'Well, then,' I went on, 'why not give him the benefit of the doubt?'

'But how do I find out for sure if it's me he wants or any girl in a sexy outfit?'

'Well goodness, that's easy enough,' I said, gradually enjoying my role as wise mentor more and more. 'You ask him. In your heart of hearts you can't possibly believe he really doesn't want you, or you wouldn't have stayed with him.'

Angie still looked miserable. 'But it's not that easy to discuss such a delicate subject. Suppose I hurt his feelings?'

'True,' I conceded. 'You'll just have to broach the subject with sensitivity.'

'Sarah's right,' Sister Murdock concurred, astonishing me.

Angie still looked a little unconvinced.

'Will you do as Sarah suggests?' Sister Murdock asked.

'I – I don't know—'

Before anybody could react Sister Murdock lashed out at poor Katerina, who took the blow with nothing more than a sharp intake of breath. I began to appreciate the strength of her resolve.

'You must promise to,' Sister Murdock insisted, 'otherwise we'll be here for the rest of the morning and Katerina will be unable to sit down this afternoon.'

'All right…' Angie yielded at last. 'You win. I'll give it a try.'

A confession, or indeed any promise extracted by torture

is hardly convincing. Another truth session was over but it left me far from happy. Its outcome had been achieved by bullying rather than consensus, and it clearly indicated that there were no lengths to which Sister Murdock would not go to get her own way.

I knew that my own truth session must be scheduled for the very near future. I would then find myself in Angie's place, equally reluctant to explain my fears. I had mistakenly convinced myself that I could avoid spilling the beans by withstanding Sister Murdock's abuse, however much it hurt. But by turning that abuse against an innocent bystander like Katerina she had shown that was not necessarily an option.

It began to look as if my suffering so far had been just the tip of the iceberg.

# Chapter Fifteen

Back in my room, tidying up before lunch, I had time to reflect on how confident I had appeared to be in solving Angie's problem. I had told her that the solution was to simply discuss it with her husband, yet I hadn't had the sense to have a similar discussion with my own husband!

I sat on the bed and stared at my face in the mirror. My stay at Sister Murdock's had convinced me of at least one thing. Self-consciousness was the bane of the middle classes. There, it sounded like a fine political slogan to me. I'd been brought up to be 'nice', hadn't I? Even the sex education at school had dealt only with fallopian tubes and contraception, never with lust. And yet of lust I had plenty. I'd shown that at Lindos, though there I'd remained ashamed and appalled at the animal I'd discovered within me. Now, at last, I was prepared to accept that animal on its own terms.

I recalled how I had met Peter. I was already a trainee manageress at one of his stores in London. A huge new superstore was being built at Croydon, which was to be the biggest supermarket in Britain. I applied for a transfer there and was accepted. I assumed there would be more opportunity at a new store and I was indirectly proved right. All the trainee managers were invited to the grand opening, at which the famous Sir Peter Easton was to be present. We weren't important enough to be asked to the dignitary's lunch, but we were allowed to go along for drinks beforehand.

As Sir Peter entered the room the store's new manager introduced us as a group with the merest wave of a hand – there were too many of us to be individually named. But as Peter's gaze swept over us I noticed it flit back to me. He'd singled me out, and sexual interest is unmistakable. The famous man fancied me!

By that time he'd been swept away with the other important guests and we were left in a corner with our regulation glasses of plonk. But my eyes followed him. I noticed him decline the offered glass of wine and ask the waiter something. But the waiter was busy distributing his tray of drinks, so I made a snap decision. I broke free from our group and walked directly across the room, through the chattering guests to Peter's side.

'Did you want something else, Sir Peter?' I asked politely.

'Oh,' he said, clearly surprised. 'Yes, a mineral water, please.'

When I returned with his drink I hovered for a couple of seconds, hoping for something – I didn't know what – to happen.

'You're one of our managerial staff, aren't you?' he said.

'Yes sir,' I said, delighted he'd embarked on a conversation with me. 'I've transferred here as a trainee. We're all very excited at the new opportunities created by the store.' I was fresh from the course and that was the way they talked there. But I immediately realised how sycophantic it must sound. 'I'm sorry,' I apologised hastily. 'That must sound so trite.'

He laughed pleasantly, and at that point the organiser butted in, telling him it was time for lunch. So that was it, my chance blown. Peter glanced at his watch and turned away, then looked back at me. 'What's your name?' he asked.

'Um… S-Sarah,' I said clumsily, suddenly feeling very tongue-tied. 'S-Sarah Singleton.'

And with that he was gone. I made my way back to my own crowd, to find that no one had even noticed my disappearance. Earlier I would have wanted to gloat to the other girls that I had been speaking to the rich and famous, but now I felt so let down I just wanted to forget the whole business.

Then, two weeks later during one of my shifts, I got called to the manager's office.

'It's Sir Peter's secretary asking for you,' said the manager, suspiciously.

I picked up the phone.

'Is that Sarah Singleton?' came a female voice.

I said it was, and to my horror she informed me that Sir Peter wanted to talk to me. I had to put a hand on the desk to steady myself.

'Sarah?'

It was him.

'Yes?' I squeaked.

'It's Peter Easton here,' he said.

'Yes,' I squeaked again. 'I know. I hope you enjoyed your mineral water.' I cursed myself under my breath for saying something so dumb, but it was the only thing that came to my spinning head.

He chuckled and told me that he did, and then – major shock – invited me out to dinner!

'Are you still there?' he enquired when I didn't respond.

'I… um… yes…' I eventually managed. 'I… I'd love

to…'

For the next few days I was an absolute nervous wreck, but fortunately the moment I got inside the restaurant I conquered my fears. Without wanting to sound conceited, it was clear that I was one of the most striking girls there. When Peter rose from his seat to greet me the look in his eyes said everything. The battle was won, the future predetermined.

# Chapter Sixteen

The previous day I had been vaguely thinking that I might brave another post-lunch encounter with the gardener and attempt to make him let me out of the grounds as well as the house. But realistically I doubted whether he had the ability. The imposing gates looked to be electronically controlled, and it seemed extremely unlikely that he would have access to those controls. Besides which, Wednesday evening's entertainment now included a trip up to Soho for a little experiment in exhibitionism to satisfy Amarinda's peculiar love of male adulation.

Or was it mine?

I recalled, with a sudden lurch of butterflies in the stomach, that Sister Murdock had me pencilled in to do an act, too. Would I really go through with it? Well, we'd just have to wait and see. If I chickened out at the last moment there was no way Sister Murdock could force me to keep my side of the bargain – not in a public place.

So for the moment I decided not to attempt another escape.

That afternoon I decided to keep out of Sister Murdock's way, and I was wandering round the house when I saw Freya listening outside a door. There could be no doubt about it; she was standing stock still, head cocked a few inches from the door of what I knew to be a sort of storeroom.

So far I'd had little to do with Freya. The most striking thing about her was that she wore glasses that made her look serious and academic. Apparently she was a self-employed designer of ceramic tiles.

Apparently she had committed herself willingly to Athelstan Hall in the hope that the stress would liven up her creative spark. It was also rumoured that she actually relished the punishment Sister Murdock handed out so freely. She certainly looked a little kinky to me. Before I could decide what to do, whether to creep away or to watch, she sensed me there, for she looked up.

She grinned at me and then beckoned. I tiptoed over to the door and put my ear to it. What I heard was the unmistakable sound of a beating; the swish, the thwack, and the suppressed grunt of a woman. What made it so awful was the duration of the punishment. I heard at least a dozen blows fall. I looked at Freya in dismay, but she just stood with her mouth open, flinching at the sound of each new blow, suffering with the victim but also clearly enjoying what we had chanced to discover.

I was in double shock, appalled at what we were overhearing but also appalled at Freya's evident enjoyment of it. How could one possibly take such pleasure in another's suffering? But there again, the sounds the victim was making were not pleas for help. Whoever was in there was evidently accepting her punishment with good grace, and the realisation gave me a sudden tremble of sexual excitement. An image flashed unbidden to my brain; it was me taking the beating. I was tied down, a ceremonial sacrifice in full view of a raucous crowd, my naked buttocks receiving and relishing that never-ending battering. The watchers formed an orderly queue, taking it in turns to deliver one horrendous blow with a heavy leather belt. And I flinched each time at the pain, then bravely gave a curt nod to the next to show I was ready for their best offering.

But then I jerked back to the present. I was as bad as Freya. I must pull myself together.

Nervously I turned the handle and pushed the door ajar. The sight that met our eyes was thankfully far more humorous than horrific. Katerina was there, dishevelled and – and beating a carpet! The grunts we could hear were hers and were purely the result of the effort she was putting into her task. Both Freya and I burst out laughing and Katerina looked round in surprise.

'I'm sorry,' I giggled. 'We thought it was a person receiving that awful thrashing!'

She smiled at us, wiped some loose strands of hair back out of her eyes, and took a rest. 'No,' she panted, 'just me catching up on some spring-cleaning. No one else will do it.'

To hide my embarrassment I offered to make some tea, and disappeared to the kitchen. When I returned with a pot of tea and three cups the two girls were sitting by the window and Katerina was shaking the front of her blouse, trying to cool off. Freya looked up as I entered.

'We were just saying,' she said to me, 'you're having a tough time from Sister Murdock.'

'Well once or twice I've certainly felt sorry for myself,' I admitted. 'But in fact I don't think I've had anything like the abuse some of the other girls have received.'

'Oh, it's not quantity that counts,' Freya claimed. 'It all depends on the circumstances. The most vicious flicks from her riding crop during the day are nothing like so difficult to take as a ritual beating in the evening, in front of everybody.'

'You're not going to be the last again tonight, are you?' asked Katerina, with awe in her voice.

I sensed her admiration and it made me feel both excited and special. 'I don't see what choice I have,' I said. 'My whole point is that I haven't ever been late, at least, not more than a couple of minutes late. Punishing someone for being last is unfair because it sets us one against the other. I refuse to rush down to the dining room at five o'clock just so that someone else is last.'

'I wish I could take your place,' said Katerina, wistfully. 'The idea of being stretched over a table and beaten in full view of the men and the other girls is one I find quite intoxicating.'

I looked at her in amazement. She wasn't just fantasising. She stared at me, lips moist. I shifted uneasily.

'You mean, you want to protect me?' I said, mainly for the sake of saying something.

'No, no.' Katerina shook her head. 'I want to experience the beating for its own sake.'

'But… but it hurts,' I said.

'You could make it easier on yourself, you know,' Freya said.

'How?' I wanted to know what she meant.

'It's all a matter of psychology,' she said. 'You hate the idea of the other girls watching your punishment and you're afraid of breaking down in front of them. But you've got the guts to stand up to Sister Murdock. Why don't you also have the courage to enjoy the beating?'

'What on earth do you mean, Freya?' I was perplexed.

'Psyche yourself up,' she suggested. 'Welcome it. That's

what Sister Murdock was trying to tell you yesterday.'

'It's pretty damn difficult to welcome a flogging with that awful paddle,' I objected.

Katerina butted in. 'But not impossible. Freya's right, I've watched dozens of girls come and go. The one's that come off worst are the ones that fight it. Think of it as a ritual. Be proud of the fact that you're the centre of attention. Ride the pain and then enjoy the afterglow.'

Freya nodded in agreement. 'Soak the pain up. Relish it. That's the way to handle it.'

'You're both dotty,' I protested. 'It's easy for you to say that, but you're not the one who's bent over the table.'

'Katerina didn't do so badly this morning,' Freya pointed out, 'and we were all watching her then.'

I couldn't argue with that, but I just stared at them quizzically. My opinion was that they were both just plain barmy.

With that, as if to prove a point, Freya got to her feet, picked up the carpet-beater and handed it to me. 'Come on,' she urged, 'hit me as hard as you like.' With that she began to undress. When she was naked she walked over to the nearest wall and leaned forward against it.

'Is – is it true you came here voluntarily?' I asked.

'Yes it is,' she replied, 'and I'm not ashamed of that. I know I'll go home the better for it. There's no achievement without suffering. That's exactly why I know I can relish the pain; because it feeds the spirit, stirs the inner creativity.'

'You're daft,' I said, rather rudely. 'It's just pain.'

'No it isn't,' she argued. 'We're all successful here, in our own various ways. Success breeds laziness and complacency, and that in turn breeds self-contempt. You know you've shown guts this week, to stand up to Sister Murdock. You can go home proud of yourself, but not complacent. Now I want to show some guts, too. So go on, hit me.'

Intentionally or otherwise I wasn't sure, but she had made me quite angry with her dismissive remarks about the pain I'd suffered, so without warning I let go with a vicious swing, expecting her to scream with agony. She gasped, for sure, and shuddered from the shock, but no pleas for leniency escaped her lips.

'And again,' she encouraged quite simply, and infuriatingly.

'Wait a minute,' Katerina interceded. 'I want to join in.'

'Well it's your carpet-beater,' I said with heavy sarcasm, holding it out to her.

'No, no,' she smirked, making me feel stupid, 'I want to join Freya.' And so saying she also took off her clothes.

I watched in fascination. They were well matched; both tall, both with glasses, both with that academic look. And both with spectacular bodies, too.

They kissed, their voluptuous bodies moulding together with breathtaking eroticism, and I suddenly felt as though I shouldn't be there, as though I was intruding in their intimacy.

'Go on,' Freya breathed huskily, breaking away from the kiss and breaking into my thoughts. 'Hit us.'

In a slight daze I let fly with an experimental blow. It struck Katerina's bottom, but she didn't flinch. I swung again.

'Mmmm,' I heard. 'That's good.'

I felt strangely angry and the third blow was much

harder. It struck firm flesh and I heard the hiss of escaping breath, but the two girls continued their slow writhing, still kissing, still engrossed with each other. And I found I was experiencing a very unfamiliar emotion – envy.

'Wait there,' I said, hoping to sound authoritative, suspecting I didn't. I ran out of the room and down the corridor. I was looking for anyone who could lend me a hand; Elspeth, Astrud, any of the girls. In the event I encountered Pearce in his weird frog mask and virtually dragged him by the hand in my eagerness. Back in the storeroom we found Katerina and Freya still engrossed in each other.

'Just a minute, Pearce,' I said, handing him the carpet-beater. I took off all my clothes and forced my way into the sensuous embrace. They both kissed me without jealousy.

The first blow hit my right buttock and I winced.

'It's okay, it's okay,' Freya whispered in my ear. 'Concentrate... feel the flesh... feel how my skin slides against yours... taste my kiss...'

I was aware of the shock of the next blow, but it didn't hit me, and I kissed both girls hurriedly, trying to compensate for the pain. We circled slowly and the beater continued its barrage. But a miracle had occurred. I had so willed myself into the other girls' bodies, so concentrated on the feast of cosseting flesh, that I was able to ignore the pain that came with each blow and think only of the warmth that followed.

'This is so good,' I whispered, astonished. 'I wish it could go on forever.'

The longer the blows fell the warmer they each became. It was uncanny. The other two girls were breathing heavily, as I was, but this was plainly from sexual excitement, not pain.

Through spinning emotions I became aware of Pearce growing increasingly agitated.

'I have to go,' he muttered. 'If Sister Murdock finds out…'

'Just a little longer,' I said lazily. The warmth continued.

'No, I must go…' he insisted, put down the implement, and left hurriedly.

'Shall we take it in turns to be carpet-beater?' Freya suggested eagerly.

I peered over my shoulder at my bottom. New red weals had appeared that were not there earlier. How had I managed to accept them without suffering the associated pain? It was magical.

'No,' I said, 'I think this delicious education is sufficient for now. I thank you both for the inspiration and example you've shown me. I hope I'll still be thanking you after this evening's punishment.'

# Chapter Seventeen

By five-thirty Katerina was back in her office. I didn't know what to say to her. An afternoon spent embracing each other and here we were again, mistress and servant. Mercifully the phone soon rang and Peter was on the line.

'Good news,' he said. 'I've completed my business and I'll be home this time tomorrow.'

'Thank goodness,' I sighed. 'Will you pick me up?'

He said he would of course, asked briefly how I was, and then was gone.

Was I really contemplating displaying myself in a Soho sleaze club that very evening? What a strange hold the environment of Athelstan Hall had over me. I'd done my bit fighting Sister Murdock, so why didn't I just phone Kendrick and go home and wait for Peter like a good girl? But I'd just arranged for him to pick me up straight from the airport, so he'd expect me to be there. I'd better not do anything unexpected, or I might risk revelation. Come to think of it, could I trust those around me not to blow the gaff when Peter arrived? Somehow I believed I could, but without any clear justification other than the feeling that they all seemed to be guilty of some sort of deception, just as I was.

It had been a short phone call and I walked without thinking to the dining hall. It was still only about five forty-five, but everyone else was already there.

Sister Murdock was watching me as I took my place at

the table, and once again I felt that surge of trepidation when faced with the prospect of pain. Four blows from that infernal paddle.

Once the girls had eaten – and I'd picked uncomfortably at my plate – Sister Murdock called for silence.

'Well, well,' she said, 'the whole group was early tonight. That's very fortunate because we have another mini event following this one. Amarinda and Sarah will be accompanying Lance, Pearce and myself up to Soho for a glimpse at the seedier side of life. Depending on the success of the trip it may very well be possible to add this peculiar form of discipline to our curriculum. I will let you all know in due course. But before that we have to discharge tonight's punishment. Sarah, I believe the honour is again yours.'

With a deep breath I prepared myself and leaned forward over the table, awaiting my submersion into the soup of pain.

The first stroke fell and I felt only a mild disappointment. Was the old witch pulling her punches? The experience was a non-event; I had done it all before. The taste of pain was in my mouth, of course, but I was used to its flavour. I glanced up at the faces lining both sides of the table, and caught Freya's gaze. She gave me an encouraging nod and I smiled back proudly.

'Thank you, Sister Murdock,' I said, without letting my voice waver. 'But I'm sure you can hit me harder than that.'

This time I heard her grunt with the strain of the swing. But I stoically gripped the side of the table, gritted my teeth, and shook my head disparagingly. 'That was a little better,' I said dismissively, 'and I thank you for your efforts, but I have to wonder whether you are perhaps beyond punishing me now.'

Freya reached forward and laid a hand over mine. It was as if I could feel her strength flowing into me. For a moment I thought we had a mingling of souls – a mystic encounter.

Sister Murdock lashed out angrily, my intentional goading clearly riling her, but I simply thought the pain through. It was there, I understood its message, but I treated it as a friend. Three of the strikes had already gone, and the punishment would soon be over.

I heard Sister Murdock breathing heavily.

'Spike,' she hissed, 'you do the last one,' and she handed him the paddle.

I was gripped with a sudden fear. I'd pushed my defiance too far. How hard would he be able to lay on the instrument of pain? Surely Freya's magic couldn't suppress the intent of a muscled and eager man such as he. I could feel my insides beginning to liquefy. The pain I was experiencing suddenly became real at last. I had sentenced myself to this nightmare through misplaced bravado.

But wasn't this actually a capitulation by Sister Murdock? She had hit me with everything she'd got, and I'd taken it. I must not let the triumph slip away.

'Am… am I to understand you accept defeat, Sister Murdock?' I managed, despite the tightening of my throat. 'That you have relinquished your task? If so, I am disappointed that you should have given up the struggle so easily.' I waited anxiously, hoping my words would have the required effect.

And they did!

She angrily snatched the paddle back from Spike and

swung at me with little finesse. It was a swift assault and my defences were temporarily down, and try as I might I could not quell the moan that escaped my lips, marring the fine show I had put on so far. I closed my eyes in exhaustion and waited for the pain to ebb. But it seemed as if it never would. For a while, as I lay there trying to get my breath back to normal, I felt as though the pain I had successfully suppressed over the first three strokes had simply stored itself up till the last, waiting to taunt me for my ill-advised goading. Wave after wave of agony swept over me, making me shudder uncontrollably. The bitter taste in my mouth was now one of defeat. Why had I been so stupid as to taunt Sister Murdock?

Amarinda and I were both very nervous on the journey up to London.

'I mustn't be recognised,' I kept saying. 'I'd rather give the whole thing a miss than risk that.'

'It's all right,' said Sister Murdock patiently. 'We've got someone coming round from one of the West End theatres to sort you out. Your own mother won't know you.'

The truth was that now the event was about to happen I was appalled at what I had entered into. I was proposing to stand on a stage and take my clothes off in front of what would almost certainly be a drunken and unruly audience. And for why? Just to prove I had the nerve! Where was the sense in that?

I turned to Amarinda. 'You got me into this,' I accused.

'No, it was entirely your idea,' she said. 'I wish I'd never mentioned anything about it.'

'But you told me you enjoyed it,' I said.

She shrugged. 'Perhaps I was wrong. It all happened without my thinking, that first time. I didn't have time to be scared. Now I'm petrified and it's all your fault.'

When we got to Soho I was horrified at the appearance of *The Good Ship Venus*. I hadn't expected it to be a high-class venue, but this was a sleazy street in a sleazy neighbourhood, and the place looked cheap and dangerous. Mercifully, Lance and Pearce had accompanied us in smart black-tie dress to look like our escorts on an evening out.

I asked Sister Murdock if she was going in with us, but she pointed out that she'd look somewhat conspicuous, which of course, she would. I put on a pair of dark glasses and the two men, Amarinda and me, scrambled out of the van and made a dash for the entrance.

Inside the general hubbub and noise was intense. Music thumped out and people were all about. To my consternation the 'stage' was actually a bar-like set-up, at which many customers were sitting, their drinks perched directly on the lights that shone upwards harshly. A girl was already strutting her stuff there, bumping and grinding to the music, inches above the faces of the men who drooled with bulging and bloodshot eyes.

The oppressively smoky atmosphere was heavy with stale alcohol and stale sweat.

'I – I can't possibly do it,' I whispered to Amarinda, the enormity of what we were doing suddenly hitting me, but to my surprise she looked amazingly calm. In fact, there was a distinctly mischievous glint in her eye that seemed to indicate that she was beginning to enjoy herself. Okay, I thought, so there was something in her soul that I didn't possess.

The seedy little manager of the seedy little club, who plainly recognised Amarinda, used his wandering hands to guide us to a squalid little changing room, where three other girls were already preparing themselves.

'Oh no,' I said, shaking my head determinedly. 'I want at least some privacy.'

The greasy manager shrugged and led us to his office. A couple of minutes later the make-up chap arrived carrying his box of paints. He set to work, and to my relief it was instantly clear that he knew what he was doing. A couple of cleverly attached pieces of latex and my face was a subtly different shape. A blonde wig and tinted contact lenses completed the illusion. I began to relax, just a little, relieved that my concerns about recognition had been taken seriously. It was just like wearing those dark sunglasses in Lindos; I became a different person, no one knew me, I could do what I liked and get away with it.

Just then the horrible little manager peered round the door at me. 'You're on next,' he said. 'Go out and look as though you're one of the audience.'

I began to tremble again. I had to go out there? But I forced myself to put one foot after another and soon I was back in the main bar area, standing next to Lance and Pearce. Lance surprised me by smiling encouragement and squeezing my hand. 'Knock 'em dead,' he said.

The MC, probably a failed comedian, was up on the stage talking into a mike that was set too loud; the volume grated on my stretched nerves and the occasional feedback made me physically wince.

'Now we come to the moment of the evening you've all been waiting for,' he announced with a feigned smile and enthusiasm that suggested he loathed his job, 'when we ask contestants to come up out of the audience and take part in the fun. Come on ladies! You could win yourselves a weekend in Paris for two!'

He peered around the room, and through the drifting cigarette and cigar haze his eyes came to rest on me. 'The tall blonde, there,' he said, beckoning with stubby, gold sovereign bedecked fingers. 'Are you a good sport? Do you have what it takes to get up on our catwalk?'

Lance and Pearce pushed me forward, but I resisted, and my resistance looked very authentic. Well, it *was* authentic. I'd lost my nerve again. I wanted to be anywhere rather than this grotty little club.

'Go on,' urged Lance. 'This is it. This was all your idea.'

Of course it was, and therefore I could not back out. I'd been so brave the whole week; was I going to turn to a jelly on the last stretch before home?

I staggered forward blindly towards the MC's outstretched hand and up the four steps onto the catwalk thing. No, no, no, I thought. It couldn't be happening. It had seemed so trivial in the rarefied atmosphere of Athelstan Hall.

But this was fact, not fiction. They were real randy men leering up at me.

Since the whole idea of the show was supposedly one of spontaneous exhibitionism by the club's few female punters, I had worn ordinary clothes. A pale green suit with a tight skirt had seemed ideal, but now my fumbling fingers simply could not get the buttons undone. I fumbled and fumbled till the crowd grew restless.

'Get on with it!' someone bellowed from somewhere out in the drifting atmosphere.

'Want a hand?' shouted another.

In the end, so thick and useless had my fingers become that in frustration I tore at the top till the buttons popped off. The crowd liked that. I tossed the expensive jacket into a corner and realised that by doing so I had totally captured the attention of the audience. Eyes were set firmly on the bra that tightly encased and squeezed my proud breasts, a soft white creation with delicate lace.

My fingers now attempted my skirt, as inept as an elephant trying to play a violin. Time was drifting and the masses wanted more. I returned to the bra with the vague idea of giving the punters something to occupy their eyes while I struggled with my belt. But I couldn't even unfasten the bra catch. At last, in extremis, I knelt, turned, and offered the task to the nearest punter, who avidly accepted the challenge, running his clammy hands round to the front and under the bra once he'd succeeded.

I slapped the mauling shovels away and moved, as gracefully as my trembling legs would allow, to one end of the bar-come-catwalk, letting the bra fall as I went, swinging my hips as sexily as I could.

And the comments of derision turned to cheers of appreciation. The more I struggled with my belt the more my breasts bobbled enticingly and the more rabid became the crowd.

Still the damned belt resisted. Somewhat flustered by its dogged defiance of my wishes I recalled what I had planned to do at the end of my performance. I gave up on the stupid thing and lustfully rubbed my breasts instead. I was amazed to note that, despite my apprehension, my nipples swelled treacherously.

'Give us a suck!' someone heckled crudely, provoking

a murmur of agreement and amusement.

Not really knowing what to do next I tried the stupid belt again, and thankfully it at last yielded, or perhaps it had simply broken. The skirt slid down over my hips, dragging my wispy lace panties with it, drawing ribald cheers until it dawned on me what was happening. I feverishly clawed the panties back up, but not before the appalling redness of my bottom had become common knowledge.

'What *'ave* you been up to?' enquired my tormentor.

'I'll kiss it better,' shouted another.

I was now at a loss to know what to do. Knickers, I understood, were non-removable. I'd run out of clothes, and in fact I was well overdue to get off the stage. But like Amarinda on her first showing, I just stood there, feeling numb. For the first time since I'd climbed on the catwalk I heard the music playing. I was supposed to dance and I'd completely forgotten to. So what could I do?

The only asset I had left was my bruised bottom. Therefore I must exploit it. I began to writhe in time to the music, legs apart, rump stuck out. The whistles became a cacophony. In fact, the unbridled adulation of me really sent the adrenaline rushing. I suddenly felt euphoric. I was suddenly *enjoying* myself. I was. Instinctively I massaged my bottomed, wincing in simulated pain as I did so. The faces stared at me, hot and horny. I pushed a hip in the direction of a particularly avaricious punter and he leaned eagerly forward and slapped the proffered flesh. I pouted with moist lips and sighed, feigning intense pain and pleasure. Soon I was writhing from one sweaty face to the next, roving hands desperate to add to my punishment.

And I simply revelled in the intensity of their homage.

Hands lashed out and my bottom suffered a welter of slaps, which ensured that the expression on my flushed face was not wholly one of playacting. In a daze I made my way along one side of the catwalk, and then back along the other until all the punters who were within reach – and that was now virtually everybody in the place – had grasped the opportunity to spank me.

My erotic immersion was so intense that in the end the MC had to drag me off. Despite my popularity I had overstayed my allotted time. I managed to blow a shy kiss to my adoring audience, then I stumbled down the steps and ran for the room at the back, gratefully accepting my clothes, which Lance had collected, as I went.

The frenzied roaring was still filling my spinning head. The baying crowd was chanting for more. My first and only chance to perform in a strip club and I'd shown them how it should be done.

What a sense of achievement I felt!

# Chapter Eighteen

The following morning I awoke wondering what my last day at Athelstan held in store. And then a simple realisation dawned; it must surely be time for my truth session! And that could be a great deal more daunting than anything I'd thus far had to endure. What was I going to say? Could I make up some story or would Sister Murdock see through that as easily as she appeared to penetrate the other girls' defences? She would argue that I had come to Athelstan for a purpose – because I had something worrying me. I could deny that, of course, but without much conviction. The simple truth was that I was there because of my abject failure in bed with Peter. She'd love to hear that, I was sure.

Okay, look at it from another angle. That was indeed why I was there, but did I now believe I had the solution to the problem? Of course I did. Peter was too restrained and I was too ashamed – a condition induced by my behaviour in Lindos. When I went back home I knew what I had to do; drop my defences – getting seriously drunk might help – and then seduce Peter into have his way with me. Hopefully the rabid sex-slave that was the true me would break through the constraints of our rather formal marriage and our public life at Finchington Yardley. If Peter was appalled by the new me then I was lost, doomed to a married life of half-hearted, infrequent sex, condemned to living a sham. But I didn't think that would be the case. If I looked at my face in the mirror I saw a picture of innocence, but also an undeniable promise of lust. Surely Peter had seen that too?

After breakfast I could see no way of avoiding the obligatory group exercises, although the idea of a strenuous game of verbal ping-pong carried very little attraction. The conflict of minds required to score up to twenty-one was as daunting a prospect as the evening confrontation with Sister Murdock and her paddle.

But I discovered that she had a new torment in store for us. That morning we were in for a session on that weird bucking bronco machine I'd spied soon after my arrival.

I had originally been amused at the thought of playing the fool on such a fairground attraction, but play it was not to be. The whole event was a serious challenge to see who had the determination to stay on the longest.

'I'm afraid this is an exercise you have to perform naked, ladies,' Sister Murdock told us, once we were gathered in the small gym.

'Why?' I gasped, feeling uncomfortable and puzzled about what was to come.

'Otherwise it wouldn't be equal,' she replied simply.

I had no idea what she meant. It seemed highly undignified to me. The three slaves were standing impassively at the corners of the gym, staring at us. I didn't see why we should give them a free show, but Sister Murdock was adamant.

I assumed her aim was once again to submit us to the maximum embarrassment. But there was more to it than that, as I found out when it came to my turn for a practice try and I clambered onto the leather saddle, already slippery from the other girls' sweat.

I had forgotten just how sore my bottom was. As soon as the machine began its gyrations I found myself lifted up in the air to crash down painfully on the unforgiving leather. Unprepared I winced and a cry escaped my lips. I longed for the protection of an item of clothing; a pair of jogging trousers, or something. My discomfort drew a giggle or two from the other girls, but no sound came from the men, although I could feel their thirsty eyes devouring my body as it bounced and swayed this way and that on the bucking saddle.

Needless to say, never having been the greatest athlete in the world, I didn't last long. The machine swivelled round violently and I lost my sense of direction and my balance. I crashed down onto the surrounding mats, gasping for breath, and then managed to stumble to my feet.

'Right,' said the sadistic witch, 'that was just a test run for you all to see what it's like. Now we're going to do it for real.'

She divided us into two teams. I was to be the captain of one side, which included Amarinda, Astrud and Millicent. We were up against Freya's team of Angie, Jericho – the quiet girl of the group, who'd not seemed to get involved all week – and Elspeth. I won the toss and put them in to bat first.

Jericho was very strong, and despite her size she clung on for over eighteen seconds, her magnificent buttocks noisily slapping the saddle over and over again, although her haughty face revealed no discomfort.

Amarinda went next, and despite her determined expression she fell off within five seconds. Elspeth put in an equally pitiful showing for Freya's side. Astrud and

Millicent both did their best for my team but by the time it was Freya's turn we were lagging a full fifteen seconds behind.

Freya's determination was awesome. She removed her glasses and shook her black hair free before she took her place on the horse. Then she grasped the short strap attached to the saddle and nodded to Sister Murdock to start the machine. We all watched in amazement as she clung on, her body thrown about mercilessly, her rapidly reddening bottom sliding backwards and forwards on the leather. I glanced out of the corner of my eye at the men, and saw that they were all fiercely aroused. There could be no doubt that this was one of the foremost perks in their week at Athelstan, watching a succession of nubile girls submit themselves to a punishing pummelling from the inanimate horse.

At last Freya fell off, exhausted. Sister Murdock announced the result; twenty-five seconds. So we were now a full forty seconds down. We had lost, surely.

It's a silly game, I told myself, as I walked forward, the last sacrificial victim. It didn't really matter who won. I'd give it ten seconds and then take a dive.

But there were shouts of encouragement from my team, and once again I was carried forward by the excitement of an audience, however small. What was much more significant, however, was the sexual content of my forthcoming display. As I'd watched Freya's performance stirring the men I had felt that familiar excitement in my stomach. I wanted to abase myself before them, to have them stare as my breasts bounced, to have them lick their lips as my buttocks grew pink and angry. A fierce adrenaline rush flooded through me. I tried to look calm and subdued but I knew my eyes were sparkling in anticipation of the self-degradation that was to come.

I grasped the strap with both hands so that my breasts were pushed forward provocatively. I was determined to milk every last ounce of adoration from those around me.

The machine started and I almost lost it straight away as the first violent lurch all but unseated me. I desperately pulled my weight forward, taking more of it on my thighs. Then I gritted my teeth and clung to the strap as if it was all there was between me and a plummet into oblivion.

And I was becoming increasingly turned on by such a blatant display of exhibitionism.

The girls were chanting in time to the clock, but I had no idea whether I'd been on for five or fifty seconds. All I knew was that I had to beat Freya. She'd enjoyed my suffering all week and no doubt she was enjoying it now, and my only possible response was to beat her at this final hurdle.

Then the inanimate beast swung vigorously and I was in a heap on the floor. I felt sure I had not yielded, and sure enough, I found myself still holding the strap. The damned thing had broken under the strain. I waved it feebly in the air in protest.

'That's unfair!' I exclaimed, trying to ignore the aches and pains that wracked my body.

'It doesn't matter,' said Sister Murdock. 'You managed forty-three seconds, therefore your team wins.'

I got gingerly to my feet, and the congratulations from my team only served to enhance my excitement.

Sister Murdock told us we could take a shower and freshen ourselves up. Once I had and felt nicely refreshed, I wandered to the lounge, where the other girls and I relaxed quietly in the comfortable chairs. Peter would be there in just a few hours, and feeling as sexy as I did at that moment I would probably rip his clothes off during the drive home.

Thinking of my forthcoming freedom, I stared out of the window. It was a glorious day, the sort of weather that, for a few hours at least, makes Sussex preferable to St Kitts. I wondered why I'd allowed myself to be locked up in such a prison when the entire world was there, just waiting to be enjoyed.

Just then Spike walked by.

'Will you take me for a walk in the garden?' I asked, a spur of the moment thing.

We went via the office and Katerina unlocked the front door to let us out. I was feeling mischievous, and although my overriding plan was to get Spike somewhere secluded, to stop for a rest and then, while he was off guard, to snatch off the mask and see what he looked like, I was also still simmering with suppressed arousal from the bucking machine.

It did occurred to me, though, that since virtually every other encounter I'd had with the staff or the guests at Athelstan had culminated in some sort of sexual eccentricity it might seem a little dangerous wandering off alone with the man. But then, according to the rules, he was committed to act the part of my slave, and therefore couldn't do anything I didn't request of him.

In fact the weather and the garden were so beautiful and so ideally matched that in no time I put aside any ideas for skulduggery and simply concentrated on enjoying our stroll.

'If you see the gardener, tell him how much I appreciate

his work,' I said. 'I'm surprised he achieves so much, in light of his other duties.'

He merely grunted. I could see a small pond in the distance down at the bottom of a shallow depression, and I led us in that direction. Sally was feeling increasingly mischievous and it was badly timed, a highly inappropriate moment for any of her naughtiness. The Sarah in me still had some misgivings that things might get out of hand.

We reached the secluded grassy bank of the pond and I sat down. It was a warm sunny spot, and so peaceful with the birds singing and insects buzzing as they busily went about their daily duties.

Feeling wonderfully relaxed I rested back on my arms, enjoying the tranquillity. Spike stood uncertainly by for a moment, and I sensed things might have already gone too far. The day, the weather, the surroundings and the situation conspired to provide an enticing atmosphere that I no longer had any hope or intention of resisting. I wanted this man, and he was mine to command. I would just have to trust, as I had already done so often throughout the week, that my lamentable lack of restraint would not get back to Peter's ears.

I patted the grass beside me and, having taken a furtive look over his shoulder to make sure we were alone and out of sight of the house, he sat down. A few minutes passed in comfortable silence, and then, without a word passing between us, we both lay back, our sides touching.

A few more minutes passed in silence, and then Spike turned towards me and started nuzzling my ear and hair. A strong arm crept across my stomach, the hand inching up slightly to carefully cup the underside of my breast, moulding it gently. I gave a sigh of pleasure and lay there in his arms, eyes shut, drinking in the exquisite sensations that suffused my body. I wondered if I could ever feel so content in the arms of Peter.

And then I lay submissively as he started removing my clothes and underwear, and then his own, until we were both naked beneath the glorious sun. We lay quietly for many more long minutes, enjoying the unique situation, listening to the sounds of nature and our own breathing. I reached about with my fingers till I found his hand, and then I lay in total enjoyment, knowing that such intensity of emotion as we both felt could only be described as a betrayal of Peter. I felt sadness as well as joy, but I knew our chemistry could not be overcome. Did this physical abandon imply that I would have to leave Peter, only weeks after our marriage?

Time drifted, but I should imagine we lay in that position for quite some time, before I became aware of something swelling persistently against my thigh. He lifted himself, and I showed no resistance as he gently guided me onto my front and knelt between my legs, massaging my shoulders and back with firm, authoritative strokes. He grasped my hips and pulled them into the air, all thoughts of being a slave clearly long forgotten. My cheek pressed against the grass and I was reminded of Mandy's complete surrender. Lips brushed the insides of my legs and a tongue forced itself into me. Whoever Spike was, I was now totally under his domination.

Gazing dreamily I caught sight of our shadows, sharply defined against the sloping grass bank by the hot summer sun. My insides turned to soft cream. The scene was as erotic as anything I could ever have hoped for. My silhouette was clear, on my knees, bottom raised in utter subjugation. Over me towered a figure, his angry spear an improbably large silhouette against the grass. Then, as I watched, that spear plunged forward and into me, in one deep thrust claiming the obedience and total surrender I was happy to give. With an aftershock I realised that at that moment I had surrendered my virginity to this unknown stranger.

For some seconds there was only the sound of determined groin striking sore buttocks. My remaining caution deserted me and I began to moan. And my man did not weaken. Each new plunge was harder and more passionate than the one before.

Happily I watched the shadow, and at last, pulling me savagely onto his cock, my lover climaxed, triggering my own unbelievable orgasm. He slumped exhausted onto my back, and I collapsed onto the grass aware only that I was, for the first time in my life, utterly, utterly satisfied.

# Chapter Nineteen

Somewhat sheepishly Spike and I returned to the house. He still had not offered me his identity and I could only assume the worst – that he was a hedonist who had bought himself a week of passion by playing the slave at Sister Murdock's bizarre establishment.

We had missed lunch but I was in any case far too emotionally charged to think of eating. I showered again and tidied myself up, but then decided to avoid the others by resting in my room for the remainder of the afternoon. I had to do my best to put Spike out of my mind before Peter's arrival.

Before long there was a tap on my door, and in came Amarinda, Millicent, Angie, and Elspeth.

'Sister Murdock's in a huff,' said Angie. 'She said it was time for your truth session but you were hiding from her.'

'You found me easily enough,' I pointed out.

'Oh, she's too proud to come looking for you,' said Elspeth. 'Her attitude is if you don't want her help then that's your loss.'

'If her help includes being beaten by that vicious riding crop, then I'm not sorry I'm missing it,' I stated firmly.

'Fair enough,' said Amarinda, 'but we were talking together and we figured you must have come here for a purpose. You must have wanted some sort of help. If you want us to listen to you, we'd be happy to, and you can be sure it won't go beyond this room. But if we're interfering then send us on our way.'

I thought for a while. 'You're right,' I eventually said, 'I did come here for a reason, but I'm glad to say that I believe I now know the solution to my problem. However, I can also see that my hang-up was at least in part due to events that occurred when I was seventeen, when I behaved poorly. I've never told anyone what happened, and to be honest there are parts I've been too ashamed even to think about.

'Perhaps I should now tell the full story, to kill the ghosts once and for all. Perhaps you girls will be sympathetic enough to listen without being too critical.'

'Whatever happened,' said Elspeth, 'it's now in the past. You can't change it. Get it out of your system and then get on with the rest of your life.'

And so I told them about Lindos. It was strangely therapeutic, relating all the gory details to an audience. We all, I am sure, have an incomprehensible desire to expose the skeletons in our cupboard, and paradoxically a ring of listeners strengthens the perverse enjoyment one finds in self-denigration.

Amazed at my own honesty I told them all about how Megan and I had met Simon and Piers on the beach, how we'd gone out together, and how, half-conscious, I had been taken advantage of before Megan saved me. I even described my rejection of handsome Alan in favour of Megan, and our steamy fondling while I was drunk. I explained the importance of the thong and the sunglasses, and my entrapment by Tassos and his friends, and my willing acceptance of it.

However, I was not brave enough to admit to the girls

that, against all appearances, I had survived the episode still a virgin. It just seemed too ridiculous. But I did not hide my shame at having let myself be used so, or my hour shivering in the sea because I could not bear to face Megan. And I described how, against all the odds, Megan had accepted me back and how our relationship became open and even more abandoned than it had been before.

And then I stopped.

I knew, of course, in my heart of hearts, that the story was by no means over. Megan was my first real love – that she was the same gender as me was hardly important. What was important was that with her I had discovered sex and we had lived for a blissful fortnight almost as one, telling each other our most intimate secrets and thoughts and embracing each other with the most unbridled passion imaginable. At the end of that time I then let her down most despicably. But how could I possibly tell my listeners that?

Perhaps it was the abrupt way I finished the saga, with a sort of happy-ever-after flavour between Megan and me, but it didn't ring true.

'Well?' said Elspeth, raising her eyebrows. 'Go on.'

'That's it,' I claimed, without conviction.

'I don't think so,' she pursued. 'Are you telling us you're a confirmed lesbian?'

'Oh no,' I said, shaking my head in denial, 'of course not.'

'So, what happened eventually between you and Megan?' she went on, not letting me off the hook.

'Nothing,' I said. 'We just sort of… drifted apart.'

'If I had a riding crop,' said Elspeth, 'I'd hit you at this point. You're obviously not telling us the truth. You said you'd had no affairs between the one with Tassos and the boys, which I'd call a fling rather than an affair, and your marriage to Peter. But that seems mighty unlikely to me.'

'I was very ashamed of my behaviour with Tassos and of how I'd treated Megan, even though she forgave me,' I said humbly. 'I think the whole thing was a bit of a trauma.'

'Three year's worth?' said Amarinda.

I shrugged ambiguously.

'Really?' Elspeth continued to probe. 'I'm guessing something even worse happened which you don't want to talk about.'

I shook my head.

'You're plainly lying, and the house rules here don't permit that,' Angie pointed out. 'So you must at least tell us what happened during the rest of your holiday in Lindos.'

There was no avoiding it. I had committed the blunder of a transparent lie, and I must pay for it. Or was it, perhaps, that I deliberately emphasised the lie, in the subconscious hope that they would draw the remaining truth from me?

After accepting my spree with Tassos, Megan and I were more than back to being friends; we were now lovers, too. I didn't have to hide behind any cloak of drunkenness to express my passion. Each night was a feast of physical extremes, each day an intimate surrender of minds as we became almost one being. Lindos is an absurdly romantic village, with its tiny winding streets and bright whitewashed walls, and we were both at a very impressionable age where no half-measures were possible. I'd had my wild thrill with Tassos and his friends, and I was now more than happy to spend the rest of the holiday basking in the sun in the day, drinking Retsina in the evenings, and entwining limbs at night, in love with Megan and in love with life.

But it was Megan who broke the mould.

Every day we went down to the same beach and every day young Tassos would come up to greet us, to smile and offer us a sunbed, and then to retire graciously when we refused. The first couple of days he looked at me pointedly and raised his eyebrows as if to ask whether I wanted another session. But when I failed to react he didn't persist. And for that I was very grateful.

On the first couple of occasions Megan obviously found his presence disconcerting. 'How can you smile at him?' she asked. 'After what he did?'

But her continual references to what had happened didn't irritate me. I could see she was eager to gossip about it, just as the two of us gossiped about everything else. I didn't want to be drawn, the experience was over and done with, but Megan could not leave the subject of Tassos alone.

Then, out of the blue one morning she said, 'You're lucky, having got it over with.'

'Got what over with?' I said, not sure what she was on about.

'Losing your virginity,' she said bluntly.

I had lied to her about that on the spur of the moment, and I now couldn't see any easy way of admitting the truth. Thankfully my sunglasses hid the guilt I knew was evident in my eyes.

'Do you think he fancies me, too?' she went on conspiratorially, saving me the problem of having to lie again.

'It would be nice to think that I'm the only girl he's ever gone with, and that he'll pine away and die from longing when I leave,' I said mischievously. 'But somehow I don't imagine that's the case. I think he'll bonk anything that moves and isn't already spoken for.'

'That isn't very complimentary to me,' she sulked.

'It's got nothing to do with you,' I said. 'He just wants as many conquests as he can notch up in a season.'

She fell silent for a while, pondering my words, and then she agreed that I was probably right. 'Are you saying I should, then?' she said, her tone betraying her eagerness, and at last it dawned on me that she was serious.

'What, screw him?' I gasped.

'Don't say it like that,' she said, pouting prettily.

'It's up to you, I suppose,' I said stiffly. 'I thought you and I had a special thing going, but I guess I can't object after the way I've already behaved.'

'It wouldn't make any difference to you and me,' she asserted. 'I just want to try it out. I want to feel it… inside me.'

But that was the end of that. She seemed to forget about it for the rest of the day. In the afternoon we even climbed up to the acropolis that overlooks the beach and soaked up some of the history, trying to imagine what life would have been like when the Knights of St John lorded it over the island. To be sure, they would not have looked down from their mountain eyrie at a beach covered with half-naked sun worshippers.

The following morning, however, and I should have been prepared for what happened.

On the beach she asked Tassos to get us a drink, after he'd greeted us as usual. I stood by, a mere observer. In fact, I found it somewhat amusing to think of Megan actually trying to lose her virginity, and I don't know why I wasn't jealous. After all, I had attracted him initially, yet he was switching allegiance without so much as a glance in my direction. And Megan, my current lover, was apparently eager to exchange my arms for his. But it just seemed that Tassos wasn't something to get upset about; he was simply a convenient sex object.

It was incredible how little encouragement he needed. That one request for a drink, and the touch of fingers when the money changed hands, was all he needed to alert his sensitive antennae to the presence of a willing, bonkable, holidaying female. I'd hardly had one sip of my cola before I looked up to see them disappearing up the beach together. How long would it all take?

I'd had time to read only a single page of my book before a shrill cry informed me and the whole beach that something was up. Megan rushed out of the hut stark naked, clasping her hands pitifully over her body.

My blood ran cold. How could I possibly have been so stupid? In an instant all was clear; Tassos would have assumed that because Megan and I were friends we must tell each other everything. Therefore, to his way of thinking, if Megan offered herself to him, as she surely had, then it must be because she expected the same special treatment that I'd received.

Three eager studs – not one.

Perhaps the other two had again hidden behind the curtain and Megan had seen them. Or perhaps they had simply sprung out and gleefully pounced on her, assuming there was plenty to go round.

But poor Megan had never been put in the picture

because wicked Sally never told her the complete story. At the very least she must now assume that her friend and lover, whom she'd treated with the utmost tenderness and affection, had played upon her the cruellest trick imaginable; throwing her right into that lion's den.

And there was more. By a sorry piece of luck it happened that there was a policeman at the top of the beach, talking lazily to one of the traders. Megan ran towards him, pointing back at the hut. Out of the hut came Tassos and the two boys. The good constable strode towards them purposefully, seemingly eager to punish their woeful treatment of one of his country's paying guests. But Tassos was ready with his explanation, gabbling in Greek, his meaning as clear as day in any language.

Young Sally had to decide whether to make an ignominious run for it, leaving Megan to her naked fate. It was what I wanted to do; to pretend the whole thing had never happened. But in the end I couldn't be so cruel to my friend. Instead I ran up the beach with a towel. Tassos spied me and, predictably, included me in his loud and finger-pointing explanation, audible and visible to all observers. 'She wanted all three of us,' I just knew he was accusing. 'She enjoyed it so much she sent her friend up, too.'

I wrapped the towel protectively around Megan. 'Come away, please,' I urged, keen to leave the awful scene.

But Megan was indignant. She had right on her side and no amount of excuses in an incomprehensible tongue could possible justify the way she'd been treated. The policeman was her friend and ally.

'*Please*,' I begged.

'I won't,' she insisted, tugging herself angrily from my

attempt at a comforting embrace.

'There were three of them before,' I whispered hastily, trying to get her and me away before the situation got *really* out of hand. 'I… I just forgot to tell you…' I finished lamely.

Realisation of what I was admitting to slapped poor Megan right in the face. As far as she was concerned, in front of so many onlookers she was a laughing stock, the butt of the world's cruellest ever practical joke.

And all because Sally was such a thoughtless slut.

# Chapter Twenty

The girls left my room and I had a chance at last for a quick nap, which I desperately needed after the exhaustion of such emotional soul cleansing. But it seemed that no sooner had I fallen asleep than the loud ringing of a bell woke me. I looked at my watch – five o'clock – almost time for Peter's arrival. Flustered, I leapt to my feet, checked my appearance quickly in the mirror, and hurried downstairs to find out what was going on.

I found that everyone had gathered in the main hall, and that Sister Murdock had rung the bell in order to call a special meeting. I looked around and noticed that we once again had four slaves in attendance. Someone had recovered Rod's eagle mask. Then I looked more carefully at its wearer and realised that Rod himself was back among us. Had his love spree with Mandy only lasted those few days?

Except… Mandy was there to, hovering beside him.

Sister Murdock banged on the table for silence.

'I'm glad to see that everyone is with us,' she began. 'Most of you will be leaving tomorrow morning. However, one or two will be leaving tonight, and I would not like to lose their presence without calling you all together to congratulate you on a busy and rewarding week.'

Her eyes searched the audience until they found me. Then she went on. 'One of our guests in particular, Lady Sarah Easton, has had a heavy and bewildering time with us, and she would not be human if she didn't feel that my treatment of her has been both unfair and unnecessarily harsh. Well, unfair is entirely true. Harsh is a matter of opinion. As I warned you all at the beginning of the week, your stay here is only worthwhile if you suffer stress, pain and embarrassment, but then rise above it. Lady Sarah has done just that and has shown herself to have a strength of character that few of us, perhaps not even she herself, would have expected.'

There was a round of genuinely enthusiastic applause and I felt proud enough to think that maybe, after all, it had been worth all the effort.

'In fact,' she was saying, 'you've all had a rough time in one way or another, both guests and staff. The only person who has come through the week unscathed is me, the chief perpetrator of all acts against you. I could let you all go home without rectifying this, but then you'd almost certainly harbour a grievance against me, which would not be healthy for any of us.'

She paused, allowing her words to sink in.

'Today, you may recall,' she went on, 'is the day when the ritual punishment for our last arrival was to be six of the best with the paddle.'

With something of a shock I realised that I had been the last to enter the hall in response to the bell. She couldn't seriously be intending to thrash me for that, could she, when I was only minutes away from being rescued by Peter?

'Lady Sarah, would you get the paddle for me, please?' she said, staring pointedly at me.

With hatred welling up in my stomach, but determined to maintain my dignity, I walked without complaint to the mantelpiece, retrieved it, and carried it back to the table. This was miserably unfair.

But, to my great surprise Sister Murdock stretched forward over the table in an inviting position.

'Go ahead,' she said. 'You may extract your revenge.'

The loathing was there enough to act upon what she offered. But my civilised conditioning was far too strong. I simply could not beat the lady. No matter how badly she had behaved and no matter how weird and kinky her ideas, I was revolted by the notion of hitting her. There was a long pause while everyone stared at me, and in the end I threw the paddle on the table.

'I'm not an ogre,' I said. 'You're too old for this sort of treatment, even if you think you want it.'

'That is a fair observation,' she said sagely. 'And that is indeed one of the remarkable characteristics of this gathering. You are all young – not one of you over thirty – and yet here I am in your midst, many years your senior. Perhaps, Lady Sarah, you think of me as an old witch playing juvenile games. But then, perhaps things are not exactly as they seem.'

With that, and to my not inconsiderable horror, she lifted her nun's habit over her head and dropped it to the floor. But my eyes were not greeted with the sight of an elderly body, but rather that of an extremely attractive woman, dressed in unbelievably provocative underwear; black bra, black satin panties, suspender belt and sheer stockings.

'Are you ready to hit me now?' she asked, breaking the stunned hush that had settled amongst the girls and me.

I snatched up the paddle with a will, but then caught sight of her face. The make-up I had noticed earlier now took on a different significance. 'First I want to know who you are,' I demanded.

'And so you shall,' she said, amusement in her eyes and in her tone. And with that she plucked at her cheeks and pulled the latex coating away from her face. 'You've no idea what a relief it is to get this thing off,' she said.

It gradually fell away while I watched, totally fascinated and amazed. But it was not till she pulled off her grey wig and let her blonde hair fall free that I recognised her.

It was Susanna Monk, Peter's actress friend!

Here was someone who had every reason to resent my success and me. And what a perfect revenge she'd had for me beating her to becoming Peter's wife. Now at last I was ready for some mayhem with that paddle!

'Get over that table, Susanna,' I hissed menacingly.

So impatient was I to hit her that I swung almost before she was down, striking the black satin of her panties with an immensely satisfying *thwack*. I heard her shocked gasp and then a strangled choke as she managed to hold back the cry of pain. Pure unbridled enjoyment welled up inside me. How sweet revenge was.

But why was I beating her through a layer of material, however delicate, when she had taken great delight in hitting me on bare flesh? And her degradation would not be complete unless it was a man who stripped her. I looked around and saw Spike.

'Pull her knickers down,' I ordered.

Dutifully he obliged. Her skin was already a fetching pink from the first blow and there were still another five to go. I prepared for my second strike.

'Wait,' she said.

I paused. She gripped the sides of the table, pressed her cheek against it and then began to moan, growing gradually louder. The sound was unmistakable. *She* had been the performer on the tape she played us on the first night! She was an accomplished faker of orgasms, no doubt – unless, as she said, the recording was made with her knowledge when she was in bed with some man. Anything now seemed possible in that bizarre house.

I let her work towards a climax and then I lashed out again. The whole table moved from the ferocity of my attack. Her voice, far from expressing a cry of pain, gave the unmistakable rhythmical groan of a woman pushed to the point of orgasm.

'Thank you, darling Sally,' I heard her mutter. 'Again, please. Quickly.'

It's funny how the subconscious part of your brain keeps on thinking even when you're fully occupied or even, as in my case, when you're overflowing with anger. Susanna Monk! That was why she had decided to play the part of a *nun*. Someone with better crossword skills than me might well have spotted that clue earlier in the week.

My third blow was so hard it made my hand sting. Goodness knows what it felt like from Susanna's position. Her buttocks were now a savage red, and I found myself giving a smile of sheer pleasure as I looked at them. But from her lips came the undeniable sound of pure ecstasy as the pain I had inflicted pushed her over the brink into never-never land.

Then my distracted thoughts of reason pushed their way back to the fore. Susanna was a busy and successful actress. So Sister Murdock's House of Correction had to be a one-off venture for her, and it was inconceivable that she had done this for any other reason than to spite me personally. That could only mean that the whole show had been put on for my benefit. All the staff and guests were actors and actresses, with me – the central character – the only one who'd been playing it for real!

And there was another problem nagging away; although she was a successful actress, with all the wealth that can bring, would she really devise such an expensive and elaborate charade simply to spite me? What the hell was *really* going on?

Still standing there with the paddle in my hand, I began to feel very unsettled.

If all this was being played out to a prepared script then this final denouement was also part of that plan. Was it the intention that Peter should arrive, be let in by Katerina, and then witness what I was doing? What would he think of what he saw? What sight would I make for him, I wondered, as I thrashed her defenceless flesh?

Expecting him to come through the door at any moment, and feeling utterly defeated and deflated, I handed the paddle to Spike and said to Susanna, 'I think I'd rather leave it for Peter to give you the remaining three blows…'

Occasionally in our lives we make astonishingly lucky blunders. The importance of this one was so great that it regularly takes my breath away just to think back on it and to see how extraordinarily fortunate my chance remark was.

'And it'll be a pleasure,' said the voice from within Spike's mask – and that voice was unmistakably Peter's!

It was another sizeable piece of luck that my face was lowered, the whole magnitude of the revelations making me feel weary, so he couldn't see the shock on my face, or recognise the dreadful secret that I hadn't realised it was him making love to me beside the pond.

He removed the mask, then apologised to Susanna, saying the other participants would never forgive him if he didn't expedite the final three strokes that were due to her.

Meanwhile, I was able to collect myself and reflect on just how naïve I had been. Peter had never gone to Japan and had never phoned me from there, and was clearly a part of the whole plan.

I was snuggled up against Peter as we drove back in the Aston Martin. I had said goodbye to all my new friends at Athelstan Hall, carefully playing the part of the trooper who had really guessed all along that things were not exactly as they seemed to be, but who had been prepared to go along with it as a good sport.

'Is this the way the rich always live?' I asked him. 'I don't think I'll ever trust anyone I meet ever again.'

'An occasional scam is good for the soul,' he chuckled. 'Though we've never set up anything as elaborate as this before. You see, the trouble with being a public figure is that you can't even pick your nose without someone reporting the fact in the papers the next day. A secure house like Athelstan is a great boon. It allows you to let your hair down in the mildest or the wildest way. I can trust all the people who were there involved.'

'So who owns the house?' I asked.

'It used to be a remand home for young male offenders,' he told me. 'That's when all the bars were installed, and accounts for the institutional bathrooms. Then it was bought by a friend of mine, but he's always abroad and he's never yet lived in it, as far as I know.'

'And were all those beatings really necessary?'

'I must admit that was largely Susanna's idea,' he disclosed. 'A few years ago I seriously considered asking her to marry me – she's a remarkable woman – but I decided she was just too kinky for her own good. But having said that, in a strange way she has a point; although few people actually enjoy being beaten, it does concentrate the mind spectacularly.'

I pondered his words for a while, gazing out at the passing countryside as we went.

'And the stories the girls told,' I eventually continued. 'Were they all made up?'

'Totally fabricated yarns, I'm afraid, except for Amarinda and poor Elspeth. Amarinda's story was originally true, but unfortunately she has already taken the plunge, thrown up her devoted husband-to-be, Runji, and immersed herself in the world of stripping for money. Her fear and excitement were pure playacting. She's her own boss, but she has few real friends and I'm beginning to think the initial thrill of what she's doing has long since worn off, even though she's only been at it for a couple of months. Your suggestion that she should have married Runji and then fulfilled her craving for exhibitionism a couple of times a year would probably have been a much better solution. Although, of course, Sister Murdock's establishment could not make that happen, as it won't exist beyond the end of this week.

'In Elspeth's case I think you pinpointed exactly what she needs to do to regain her self-respect, and to that end I'll make sure she has enough capital to start a modelling agency.'

I shook my head, recalling, often with embarrassment, all the things that had happened during the week. 'What made you dream all this up?' I asked, still barely able to believe it all.

Peter turned to look at me openly. 'I was unhappy at the way our marriage started off,' he said. 'We were both far too restrained. I talked to Susanna about it and she said that you needed to be "taught submission", to use her words. In a sense she was right – you needed to be taken down a peg or two and shown that looks are not everything. But before you get angry let me say that I think submission is a lot more subtle than that. A satisfactory sexual relationship requires that both parties let down their defences and act in an entirely different manner from the way they do in public. That's not easy, but remember how close we were by the pond earlier. Before that you were far too much in awe of me for our relationship to be one of equals.'

I could see he was right, but with a sudden flush I recalled my excesses with Astrud. 'Did – did you know in detail what was going on between me and some of the other girls?' I asked warily.

'No,' he said, 'and I don't think I want to hear now. Susanna said you need to be brought to the boil sexually. I agreed, but said I was damned if we were going to use other men to stoke the fire. But I had no objection to girls, provided I wasn't privy to the details.'

We were silent for a while as the car sped through the balmy evening. Then it occurred to me that, at least in Peter's mind, there was still some ambiguity about one incident, and I was overcome by a fit of nervous giggling. 'I can't believe the amount of effort you went to just to manufacture a situation where you could pretend to be a randy gardener!' I exclaimed. 'If you wanted me to suck you, why didn't you just ask me?'

He started laughing too. 'I will in future,' he said. 'But I was indulging myself with a little game and a lot of pleasure.'

I groaned. 'I can't believe what a lunatic I've married,' I smiled. 'None of this was necessary, you know. I am amazed you married me without realising that beneath all this beautiful respectability there lies the heart and soul of an insatiable slut.'

He shifted gear to negotiate a bend and grinned at me, a noticeable lump tenting his trousers. 'Prove it,' he said, his voice growing husky.

I looked at him with wide eyes, and slid a hand over that beckoning bulge, squeezing slightly. 'And how would you like me to do that?' I purred innocently.

He cleared his throat a little. 'I – I think you know very well how,' he croaked.

'On one condition,' I teased. 'From now on, when we're alone, you call me Sally.'

# Exciting titles available from Chimera

| | | |
|---|---|---|
| 1-901388-20-4 | The Instruction of Olivia | *Allen* |
| 1-901388-17-4 | Out of Control | *Miller* |
| 1-901388-18-2 | Hall of Infamy | *Virosa* |
| 1-901388-23-9 | Latin Submission | *Barton* |
| 1-901388-19-0 | Destroying Angel | *Hastings* |
| 1-901388-21-2 | Dr Casswell's Student | *Fisher* |
| 1-901388-22-0 | Annabelle | *Aire* |
| 1-901388-24-7 | Total Abandon | *Anderssen* |
| 1-901388-26-3 | Selina's Submission | *Lewis* |
| 1-901388-27-1 | A Strict Seduction | *Del Rey* |
| 1-901388-28-X | Assignment for Alison | *Pope* |
| 1-901388-29-8 | Betty Serves the Master | *Tanner* |
| 1-901388-30-1 | Perfect Slave | *Bell* |
| 1-901388-31-X | A Kept Woman | *Grayson* |
| 1-901388-32-8 | Milady's Quest | *Beaufort* |
| 1-901388-33-6 | Slave Hunt | *Shannon* |
| 1-901388-34-4* | Shadows of Torment | *McLachlan* |
| 1-901388-35-2* | Star Slave | *Dere* |
| 1-901388-37-9* | Punishment Exercise | *Benedict* |
| 1-901388-38-7* | The CP Sex Files | *Asquith* |
| 1-901388-39-5* | Susie Learns the Hard Way | *Quine* |
| 1-901388-40-9* | Domination Inc. | *Leather* |
| 1-901388-42-5* | Sophie & the Circle of Slavery | *Culber* |
| 1-901388-11-5* | Space Captive | *Hughes* |
| 1-901388-41-7* | Bride of the Revolution | *Amber* |
| 1-901388-44-1* | Vesta – Painworld | *Pope* |
| 1-901388-45-X* | The Slaves of New York | *Hughes* |
| 1-901388-46-8* | Rough Justice | *Hastings* |
| 1-901388-47-6* | Perfect Slave Abroad | *Bell* |
| 1-901388-48-4* | Whip Hands | *Hazel* |
| 1-901388-50-6* | Slave of Darkness | *Lewis* |
| 1-901388-49-2* | Rectory of Correction | *Virosa* |
| 1-901388-51-4* | Savage Bonds | *Beaufort* |
| 1-901388-52-2* | Darkest Fantasies | *Raines* |
| 1-901388-53-0* | Wages of Sin | *Benedict* |
| 1-901388-54-9* | Love Slave | *Wakelin* |
| 1-901388-56-5* | Susie Follows Orders | *Quine* |

| | | |
|---|---|---|
| 1-901388-55-7* | Slave to Cabal | *McLachlan* |
| 1-901388-57-3* | Forbidden Fantasies | *Gerrard* |
| 1-901388-58-1* | Chain Reaction | *Pope* |
| 1-901388-61-1* | Moonspawn | *McLachlan* |
| | | |
| 1-901388-59-X* | The Bridle Path *(Jul)* | *Eden* |
| 1-901388-62-X* | Ruled by the Rod *(Jul)* | *Rawlings* |
| 1-901388-63-8* | Of Pain and Delight *(Aug)* | *Stone* |
| 1-901388-64-6* | Sashay *(Aug)* | *Hazel* |

All **Chimera** titles are/will be available from your local bookshop or newsagent, or direct from our mail order department. Please send your order with a cheque or postal order (made payable to *Chimera Publishing Ltd*) to: **Chimera Publishing Ltd., PO Box 152, Waterlooville, Hants, PO8 9FS**. If you would prefer to pay by credit card, email us at: **chimera@fdn.co.uk** or call our **24 hour telephone/fax credit card hotline: +44 (0)23 92 783037** (Visa, Mastercard, Switch, JCB and Solo only).

**To order, send:** Title, author, ISBN number and price for each book ordered, your full name and address, cheque or postal order for the total amount, and include the following for postage and packing:
**UK and BFPO:** £1.00 for the first book, and 50p for each additional book to a maximum of £3.50.
**Overseas and Eire:** £2.00 for the first book, £1.00 for the second and 50p for each additional book.

*Titles £5.99. All others £4.99

For a copy of our free catalogue please write to:

Chimera Publishing Ltd
Readers' Services
PO Box 152
Waterlooville
Hants
PO8 9FS

Or visit our **new** Website for details of all our superb titles and secure ordering
**www.chimerabooks.co.uk**